FutureWord Publishing

Printed in the USA

02.01.2016

FutureWord Publishing
872 E. Goodman Rd. Ste. 310
Southaven, MS 38671   Fax 901-217-8514   www.futureword.net

Beautiful

THESE SUMMER NIGHTS — STORIES

JOE VIGLIOTTI

STORIES

HENNIGANS-BY-THE-SEA

He sat in the waiting room, his hands clasped between his knees. His heart was heavy, and the room smelled of the vinyl-covered cushions on the chairs. It was windowless, and clean, and cold, and bright. His hands trembled, and he felt sick, and lost, and he fought the tears that crowded in at the corner of his eyes. He couldn't let the others see him this way, couldn't let his children and his grandchildren see him as anything other than what he had always been —strong, collected, understanding.

But now he was none of those, and he couldn't understand how things had turned out how they had. People grew old, and they lost their sight, and their hearing, but they never lost the way they felt. And he knew how he felt about his wife, cold and lifeless down the hall.

He couldn't understand why it had to end. He understood that it would have come sooner or later. And he was blessed to have known her as long as he had, to have shared life with her for sixty-five years. Not many people were that lucky. Everything, he tried to remind himself, went according to God's time, where time itself did not exist.

But time existed here, in this place, in this cold, clean, and bare waiting room.

He was blessed, indeed, to have shared so much of life with her; and so very blessed that his family had remained close, and that they saw one another frequently —his two sons and his daughter, and their families.

He reached for his wallet, and pulled it out, and flipped through the photographs he kept. Every year, at every anniversary, he and his wife took a new photograph together, and he inserted that first. There were the children, and the grandchildren —and their smiles radiated warmth from the little images he'd printed from the computer.

And the last image he kept in his wallet was an actual photograph, from 1945 —the first photograph he'd taken with his wife after their wedding, on the first morning of their honeymoon. They'd met in high school; and he'd gone off to Europe to fight, and he went across the Rhine and into the heartland of Germany. He'd come home without friends, but he came home to the arms of the girl he loved. And they'd married that summer, right after he'd come back.

And he'd wanted everything to be perfect. Although he could never make everything perfect – flight delays, and flat tires, and financial difficulties early on, and stovetop fires, and no sprawling home in which to live –she'd always made things perfect, simply by being in his life.

He'd tried to give her the perfect honeymoon. They went to the ocean, to the sea, to take in the warm sun and walk across the hot sand, and to swim in the surf. And they enjoyed the night fireworks, and the bustling diners and quiet restaurants.

Their first morning there, they went to a place where her parents had gone on their honeymoon for breakfast, to Hennigan's-By-The-Sea, on the boardwalk, over the ocean. The waves danced about the great pillars which supported the walk, and the shops, and the restaurant, and they were steady and calm.

He and his wife wore the clothes they'd left in the night before. The airline had lost their luggage, but had found it, and was shipping it to them now. So she suggested they at least head out to eat, and he reluctantly agreed. He was humiliated, to be honest, that something like this would happen so soon, that he couldn't have made *everything* perfect for her.

And she asked their waiter if he wouldn't mind taking a photo of them –the photo that became the first in a long line of photographs which he lovingly kept in his wallets over the years. She was beautiful in the summer sunlight, and was smiling broadly. She told him she'd never been happier.

As happy as he was, the luggage had not yet arrived, and he couldn't muster up a smile. When they got back to the hotel, the luggage was waiting, along with a personal written apology.

When they returned home, and she had the photos developed, she didn't even mind that he hadn't smiled. She kissed his cheek and called him grumpy. And the photograph was reproduced and became the subject of dozens of dinner conversations. It was a simple story, but it was their first story together, and his wife enjoyed telling about how everything to her, at least, had been perfect.

Everyone had seen the photo. The children, and their spouses, and their grandchildren, and the friends of their grandchildren.

His wife had been so happy just to be there with him, and he was worried about the luggage, and making sure her things hadn't been lost.

What a fool, he thought, to have not smiled. How could he have not smiled? He'd regretted it every time he saw the photo. He'd hated himself for it, even. He couldn't muster a smile simply because he was with her.

He told her, once. He told her he regretted it.

But she didn't. She told him not to, but he did anyways.

Dear God, he thought, clutching the photograph between his hands now; Dear God, couldn't he go back? Couldn't he go back and change things now? Just to have smiled. Or couldn't he join her now in Heaven?

The eldest son was the last one at the hospital, and he knelt in the chapel and prayed; his tears coursed down his face. Everyone was at his parents' house –it was only his father's house, now –and he looked at the clock. It was almost one in the morning, and he figured it was time to get his father, and head home. There would be much more to do in the morning, and his father was sitting alone in the waiting room, just as he'd asked.

The son went up the stairs rather than taking the elevator, hoping to avoid anyone he didn't have to see.

He went past the room where his mother now rested; the door was closed, and the lights were long gone. He went down the hall, toward the lobby on the floor, toward the nurses' station.

"Is my father still up here?" he asked.

The nurse nodded, and pointed to the waiting room. "He hasn't left."

But as she spoke, the light in the room went out; and then it came back on, and the son and the nurse –both curious –rushed to the room, worried that something had happened.

Upon entering the room, they were surprised to find it empty. "I didn't see him leave," said the nurse. "I kept watch."

The son looked about, and it was true. No one was in the room. Perhaps his father had gone to the restroom, or to make a call?

Yet as he turned to leave, the son noticed something at the foot of the chair where his father had sat; and he bent down to pick up a single photograph. Turning it over in his hands, he was surprised to discover that it was the photograph of his parents at Hennigan's, which had always been the focus of lighthearted conversation. The ocean, and side of the restaurant, and his parents at the outdoor table with his mother smiling, and his father grimacing.

As he stood, his heart caught in his chest.

There, in the photograph that he'd seen a thousand times, where he'd seen his father frown a thousand times —there in the photograph, now, his father was smiling broadly for the first time, at Hennigan's-By-The-Sea.

THIS IS ABIGAIL

The boy behind the counter smiled at Sophie kindly enough, but she couldn't help but feel that he had already judged her. The baby kicked inside her, as if to both comfort her, and tell her that she may just be overreacting. Or maybe unnecessarily defensive. Either way, it didn't matter. She had placed her order, and now sat at a table alone, waiting for breakfast, anxious to get out and to the college. She had accelerated her high school graduation, and was now taking college courses —as many as she could.

She was anxious to eat, get out, and get to the college. She checked her cell phone to see the time, and ignored the text messages from her friends. She would reply to them later, when she had more time.

"How far along are you?" the boy behind the counter asked as he cleared off the next table over.

"Six months," said Sophie. She instinctively put her hands on her stomach. She knew the questions that would follow. She ran a hand through her dark brown hair. In fact, she knew them so well by now that she could practically predict the order that they would be asked in.

"And I'm sixteen," Sophie added. "And no, the father isn't around," she said, bitterly. Perhaps, she thought after the fact, a little too bitterly.

"I'm sorry," said the boy. "I didn't mean to pry." He looked like he was in college.

Sophie suddenly regretted sounding so defensive. The baby kicked inside her again.

"I'm sorry," she said. "I'm just used to a certain way that things happen."

"It's alright," said the boy. "I can't imagine what you have to deal with."

"You get used to it, I guess," said Sophie sadly.

"Have you decided on a name?" the boy from behind the counter asked. But the cook from the kitchen called for him before she could answer. As he turned away, another girl sat down beside Sophie.

"How far along are you?" the girl asked Sophie. Sophie was ready to sigh, loudly. Half the time, she felt so hopelessly frustrated she just wanted to cry. With finals this week, the car repair, the insurance bill coming up... it just didn't seem to stop.

"Six months," said Sophie as gently and as patiently as she could.

"But you're not going to keep her?"

This question was different. It took Sophie by surprise. She had not been asked this question, not since she found out she was pregnant, not since everyone found out she was pregnant. And she still didn't quite know how to answer. But as if to remind Sophie that she was alive, the baby kicked inside of her, and moved about quite a bit. No, thought Sophie; this is life... this is life inside me. But still... the car... the insurance... everything.

Sophie looked at the girl sitting beside her –she couldn't have been more than thirty, and so she wasn't really so much a girl anymore. Sophie looked towards where the boy had been, but he was still in the back.

"I don't know," said Sophie at long last. "I just don't know for certain."

"You don't know?" said the woman beside her. Sophie looked at her a little more closely. She was beautiful, with long brown hair and amber eyes, and looked kind.

"Do I know you?" Sophie found herself asking. "You look like someone I know, somehow."

"What about the baby?" the woman asked. Sophie was a little confused. She thought, perhaps, that the woman was a member of a prolife group, or the movement in general, and had just happened to notice Sophie in her delicate condition. Perhaps she had seen the woman at the doctor's... the baby kicked, and Sophie shifted against the backrest of the chair.

"She's awfully active today," said Sophie with a hint of a smile. She put her hands on her belly.

"So you won't have an abortion?" the woman beside her asked pointedly, but gently.

"No," said Sophie. "I don't think I will... I mean... I thought I would... but then I couldn't... I prayed, and I couldn't... I talked to my parents. I could still have it done now, but I don't think I will. I'm fairly confident."

"That doesn't sound *too* confident," said the woman.

Sophie frowned. "No," she admitted. "I don't suppose it does."

"I don't think you should," said the woman. And she added, perhaps as an afterthought, "I'm a lawyer."

"Are you offering me legal services?" asked Sophie. "I'm confused."

"I'm just telling you what I've done with my life," said the woman with a smile. "My mother was sixteen when she had me. Now I'm married, I've begun a family, and I try cases in constitutional law relating to the prolife movement." The baby shifted around inside Sophie.

"I don't think you should have an abortion," said the woman. "I know it'll be beyond difficult, but you can't justify how the absence of one life might forever impact, or change the world."

Sophie was quiet for a moment. She quite honestly didn't know what to say; but the boy from behind the counter appeared with Sophie's food, set it down, and retreated back into the kitchen at the call of the cook.

"You won't have an abortion," said the woman. "In your heart, you know you won't." The woman said it so kindly and gently that Sophie couldn't help but smile.

"And you'll be a wonderful mother," said the woman. "I know you will be."

Sophie was again taken aback; and the baby seemed to stay still with the comfort that the woman had shown her mother.

The woman stood. "I have to be off," she said as the boy emerged from the back once more. "God will take care of you," said the woman. "You have nothing to fear for long."

"What is your name?" Sophie asked the woman, eager to know who it was that had spoken with her. The woman turned to go.

"You'll name me Abigail," said the woman. "It's been in your heart all along."

Sophie turned towards the front of the diner, eyes narrowed, brow furrowed, and looked at the clock behind the counter. She was beyond confused now. Turning back to the woman for clarification, Sophie found the woman was not there.

She spun around on her stool, but the woman was not behind her. She was not visible through the glass on the sidewalk.

"Looking for someone?" asked the boy.

"Yes," said Sophie. "What happened to the woman that was sitting here with me? Did you see which way she went?"

The boy looked around. "What woman?"

"The one who was sitting here beside me when you brought me my food," explained Sophie.

"She must have left before I got out here," said the boy. "There wasn't anyone out here when I brought your food out."

Sophie was stunned into silence. What had just happened? *What in the name of God had just happened?* She knew she wasn't crazy; the woman had been there, right beside her. *The woman had spoken to her.*

"I think I just met my daughter," said Sophie quietly. The baby kicked happily inside of her, and Sophie looked at the boy. His face was kind, and he looked as though he didn't think she was crazy. He didn't seem to have heard her. And she smiled.

"I'm John," said the boy, offering Sophie his hand, which she grasped. His touch was warm, and gentle.

"I'm Sophie," she replied. "It's nice to meet you."

"And you," said John. He smiled; hesitantly, perhaps, he pulled out his cell phone. "I know this may seem sort of random... do you think I could have your number?" His face turned just a little red.

"Of course," said Sophie, smiling, and taking out her own cell phone.

"And who is this?" asked John, gesturing towards Sophie's stomach.

And Sophie smiled, and looked at John, and said quite proudly, "This is Abigail."

THE CAMP LIKE HEAVEN

"The soldiers come, and they take everything."

The observation was nothing new to Mosi. He watched his little brother, hands in pockets, kicking at the dusty ground. He wandered in a small circle, head hung low, eyes scanning the ground around him, as if looking for something lost.

"Sit down, Olwenyo," said Mosi. "Better to sit down than tire yourself out."

Olwenyo stopped his pacing, looked up at his eleven year-old brother, and shook his head. "They take everything."

Mosi looked up and down the dusty street, surveying their small kingdom of ruins from atop a small pile of decimated brick. At the far end, a wrecked car burned; the sun-baked buildings were riddled with bullet holes. Torn papers were whisked along in the dry wind. Anything of value was gone, taken by one militia group or another to fight the other. And Mosi and his brother Olwenyo were left behind.

"If Father was here," declared Olwenyo, "they wouldn't take everything."

"Sit down," said Mosi. "Father went off to fight with them. He will not come back. Now it is us, it just us left here."

They had come back from across the city, had come back where workers in bright clothes had given them something to eat, and more to bring home with them. But the militia had come through in their clunky, tan jeep, and had taken everything. So it had been for years. So it would be for more. And how long would it be before the workers in bright clothes went home, and stopped giving them food?

Mosi sat up straight. There was a sound on the wind, an echo through the alley. He turned, and listened. Footsteps. Bounding footsteps. He turned to Olwenyo and yelled, "Quick! Hide! The militia is coming back!"

Olwenyo scrambled across the street to his brother, and Mosi forced him down behind the pile of rubble upon which he sat. He jumped behind, and peered over the top, could hear his own haggard breathing, hot and dry in the dusty wind.

Quiet. Footsteps. Lots of footsteps in the alleyway across the street.

"How many are there?" Olwenyo asked.

"I cannot tell!" whispered Mosi. "Now hush!"

The footsteps drew near, and then Mosi saw the small, dark form emerge across the street from the alley. Chinaza came running through the street, bounding among the twisted tires and bits of trash.

"Chinaza!" yelled Mosi, standing once more. "You nearly scared Olwenyo to death!"

"He did not," protested Olwenyo, but Mosi ignored him.

"There is another place I have found!" shouted their eleven year-old compatriot. "I have found another place! I have been there all morning, since the sun came up!"

"You were not at the food camp," said Mosi. "You missed breakfast."

"I have found an even better place! And I have been there all morning," said Chinaza, coming to stand at the base of the rubble. The sweat glistened on his forehead in the scorching sunlight, and his drenched shirt clung to his back as he climbed the crumbled bricks.

"Where have you been?" asked Mosi, sitting down beside him. Olwenyo climbed up and sat beside them, holding his knees in his hands and lifting his feet up off the hot rubble.

"To the most wonderful place," Chinaza, his eyes wide. "I found it quite by accident, but I know that I can find it again. I learned the way. I went there this morning, and took a wrong turn, but it was the greatest wrong turn I could have made. It is another camp that I have found, a camp like Heaven.

"There is plenty of food. They give you rice, and meat, and fresh, clean, cold water. It is the most wonderful water I have ever had. You can sit down, and eat, and you can go back for more if you are young. And you get there, and they invite you in, and you stand in the line, and they give you food. And they look you in the eyes and smile, and ask you how you are doing. At the other camp, they serve you, but they do not ask how you are. But they asked me at this camp. And they have men with guns who protect you at this camp, with great big guns and tan uniforms. And they will play soccer with you.

"And they will sit down and eat beside you, and they offer you food to take back; and I told them I had hungry friends named Mosi and Olwenyo, and they told me to bring you back. And they have more food, and medicine, and doctors who will take care of you."

At this, Chinaza raised his arm, and proudly showed them his bandaged elbow. "When I hurt it yesterday playing, I thought it would bleed forever, and I would die in the street. But today, they saw my elbow, and cleaned it, and put medicine on it, and bandaged it."

Mosi waved Chinaza off. "There is no such place," he declared. "God is not here in this place. You must have been dreaming in the sun. At the camp we go to, they give you food and medicine if you need it."

"Yes," said Chinaza. "But this place is much, much different."

"Such a place does not exist," Mosi scoffed. "No such place could exist here."

"Such a place does exist!" Chinaza professed. "And I will take you there." He stood, and began to descend the rubble. "Come! I will take you!"

"No," said Mosi. "It is not safe to go out. The soldier could come and kill us. We must stay here, and wait until the morning, and go to the camp we always go to."

"No," insisted Chinaza. "I told them I would bring you back. And I mean what I say!"

"You were sun dreaming!" said Mosi. "The sun has certainly rotted your head."

"I know what I saw," said Chinaza. "I know what I ate." He held out his arm to show them his bandaged elbow once more. "They put this on me!"

"Let's go," said Olwenyo. "I would like to meet these people."

"Nonsense," said Mosi. "The militia would kill us like they killed Mama. The only safe way is to our familiar camp."

The sound of an engine interrupted their argument, coming loud and down the dusty street. All three children looked off in the same direction, just in time to see a tan jeep careen around the corner,

25

packed with militiamen, with guns and missiles. Before them ran a single man, a loaf of bread tucked beneath his arm, running down the street, running towards the pile of rubble upon which Mosi stood.

"Quick! Across the street! We must go!" shouted Mosi. "We must hide!"

The militiamen opened fire, and their guns sounded like a thunderstorm, the sounds shrilly echoing off the walls. The man ran, and the militia fired, and the three boys charged down the rubble.

They kept firing, and the man screamed, and the bread flew through the air, landing at Olwenyo's feet as he raced across the street. Mosi could hear the shouts of the militia behind them: "Kill his children! They are stealing from us!"

"We have stolen nothing!" shouted Mosi into the sky as he followed Olwenyo and Chinaza through the alley across the street.

"Quick!" shouted Chinaza. "This way!" He darted left as gunfire erupted in the alley behind them. Bullets thudded into the mud walls over their heads, and they scrambled left and then right.

"We must lose them!" shouted Mosi.

"We will!" yelled Chinaza. "Just stay with me!"

They scrambled over bricks and dodged trashcans, ducked as shots rang out, and headed down side streets covered in graffiti. "This way!" shouted Chinaza, and suddenly the next alley opened up into the middle of a wide street. They sprinted across the hot, sandy road to see the militia jeep speed around the corner. Looking back behind them, they could see the gunman on foot still pursuing them. He opened fire, and chunks of brick dislodged and fell from the building beside them.

They raced through the next alley, and onto the next street, and the jeep turned the corner. Looking left, they found no alley, no way out. So they sprinted down the center of the street, heading toward the next intersection, Chinaza in the lead. The men in the jeep opened fire, and Chinaza darted into a small alcove, in which rested the broken-down door to someone's house.

Mosi scrambled in after Chinaza, and turning back, he saw Olwenyo scream as he fell into the alcove. He rolled over, grabbing at his leg, and Mosi's face flushed. The blood was pouring from Olwenyo's leg, the same as it had from their mother's months before. He dropped to his knees and grabbed his younger brother, pulling him back into the alcove, watching the trail of blood that soaked out into the sand.

"No!" shouted Mosi. "You must not be shot!"

Olwenyo was crying, holding his leg, grasping it, eyes shut tight. "I don't want to die," he sobbed. "Please, Mosi, please! Take it out of my leg! It is bleeding!"

There was more gunfire in the street, and there was a loud explosion that shook the building by which they hid, and then there was silence, except for Olwenyo crying.

And then Mosi froze. Out in the middle of the street appeared a single man, in a tan uniform with a large gun aimed down the street. And then there was another, and then another, and then another. And they moved forward slowly, looking this way and that, carefully, slowly. And one of them glanced toward the alcove, and lowered his weapon.

He came toward them, gun in hand, and Olwenyo stopped crying, terrified. The man came up to them, and dropped the gun to his side, and then yelled over his shoulder.

"Thompson! Get Peters up here, *now!*"

Another man showed up beside the first, and they knelt down without the guns, and the second man spoke.

"We're not going to hurt you," he said, hands open and outstretched. "But your friend here is hurt, and we'd better take a look at him."

It was the language of the men at the camp. Mosi knew enough of it to understand. And he nodded.

"Brother," he said.

"We're going to help your brother," said the first man. The second man inched forward, and pulled from a bag at his side some sort of package, some sort of white powder which he sprinkled over Olwenyo's leg, and Olwenyo cringed and gritted his teeth. "This will help until we get back to the camp," he said. "Luckily, the bullet only skimmed his leg. But it's still bad." He pulled out a bandage, and carefully wrapped it around Olwenyo's leg.

A great tan jeep with a roof and gun on top pulled up in the road, and the second man lifted Mosi's brother up into his arms. "Let's go, boys," he said. "To the camp."

Chinaza stood and went out into the sun immediately, but Mosi remained where he was in the shadows, uncertain, afraid. The first man remained kneeling.

"We're not going to hurt you," he said. "I promise. You can see for yourself, if you'd like." He stood, and stepped back, and pointed down the road. Mosi went forward, and peered around the corner of the building to see the militia jeep burning, and the militiamen motionless on the ground in the kingdom of ruin.

And Mosi stepped out into the hot sunlight, and watched the men in tan uniforms help his brother into the jeep, and watched Chinaza wave him on. "These men will take us to the camp I told you about!" he exclaimed. "The camp like Heaven! Quick! We must go!"

Mosi walked beside the man to the jeep wordlessly, and as he went inside, Mosi looked back at the man. And suddenly, he understood.

"God is in this place," he whispered to himself. And then to the man, he asked, "Who are you?"

The man smiled, and it was a kind and reassuring smile. It was a smile of honesty, and of friendliness.

"Americans," the man said. "We're Americans."

THE NIGHTMAN

I always ate dinner late at night at Third Place, a diner on the corner of Second and West. I ate there every night, Monday through Friday, of every week, of every month. I'd been eating there at Third Place since before we charged up San Juan Hill after President Roosevelt in the summer of 1898. I was right behind the T.R. when we crested the summit, and I saw the sun ignite Old Glory in brilliant colors against the sky. I'll never forget that day.

Since the war, though, things hadn't been quite the same. I don't have the same taste for food that I used to. Sometimes I feel like I'm just not hungry at all, but then again, it doesn't surprise me too much. I had been eating there for years, and sometimes, you just lose taste for certain meals. But I was too comfortable to find any place new.

Or maybe it was from the war. War changes things, you know. Such as your taste for food. I was a nightman before the war in Cuba, and I guarded a bank until dawn. I heard about the war, and then about Teddy forming his First Volunteer Cavalry – later known as the Rough Riders –and I joined up. I rode the train to Texas, where the unit was being formed. It was only the second time in my life I'd been on a train. The first had been when I went to Gettysburg with my father for a reunion of his regiment.

Even the memories seem faded now, tasteless even. War changes everything. Time, perception... even your understanding of human existence is changed, and you realize just how frail and delicate a human life really, truly is.

As soon as one war ends, another begins. The people who think every war will be the last war are always wrong. Not everyone is as free as we are.

When you experience the grisly remains sprayed across a smoke-studded battlefield, you wonder yourself how there could ever be another war when so many people are dead, and when there is such a terrible magnitude of destruction. But perhaps that is God's punishment to those of us who take to war: there will always be another war until we are either all free, or until we are all dead.

War hit Harry Spencer pretty hard.

They called this one World War II. It was ironic, because the Great War –the First World War – was supposed to end everything. It was to be "the war to end all wars". It ended nothing, except the lives of millions. God must have cried when he saw just what we were capable of.

Harry Spencer was a doughboy from that first world war. He went over with Blackjack Pershing in 1917 when the Germans wouldn't quit hitting our merchant vessels. Now we're fighting the Germans again. Harry Spencer's son went to Europe.

He came back in a box.

Losing your son has got to be a devastating thing. Or your grandson, for that matter. I wouldn't know. I never actually met my son. My wife gave birth to him while I was in Cuba, and I learned about it in a letter she sent me a few days before I was killed heading over the crest of the hill, right behind Roosevelt.

I've known Harry for years. I met him at the diner before the second war. He ate late dinners at Third Place, too, because he was also a nightman. In a way, you could say I got him the job. But he walked a lot slower now, and who could blame him?

People reach Heaven through different paths, in different ways. For whatever reason −perhaps because I was once an instrument of death −God decided that I was not prepared to move on to Heaven. So He kept me here, taking my late-night dinners, and to continue that part of my life as though it had never ended. When the daylight came, I disappeared, and was invisible to the human eye. When the night came on, I became physically-apparent, and I went to go eat.

The staff at Third Place has changed over the years. Owners and waiters have come and gone. So have the people, and the faces, but there were some regulars –like Harry –who never went. And I was friends with all of them.

I got to know everybody who worked those late-night shifts. Around eleven at night, the customers usually stop coming in; and so the Gary the cook, and the sole waitress at the hour, Marissa, usually sit with us and drink coffee. Gary, like Harry, is also a veteran of the First War. He's friendly, and his hair is mostly gray now. Marissa is a university student by daylight, and her fiancée is over on one of the islands off Japan.

One of the unfortunate things about being dead, is that you always know who died ahead of anyone else. You're bound not to pass along that information, and so I can't tell Marissa that her fiancée was killed last week in an amphibious landing. They haven't found his body yet, and they probably won't. It was pinned underneath a tank, underwater.

I remember the deserted Friday night when Harry found out his son had been killed. He was absolutely devastated. I also remember when Harry would bring in his kids –the son, and two daughters – years before the war. Jack –the son –was a good kid. He opted out of college for the Army and was attached to Patton's Third Army, and then he was transferred to command a squad of motorized infantry that took Remagan Bridge. A German sharpshooter got him there.

Jack was Harry's life. He was the best father I've ever known, and I've known a lot of them in this line of work... if you could call it that. When I was breathing, I was an instrument of death, and now that I am dead, I am an instrument of life. We, as God's agents, nudge things along in the appropriate directions. And Harry Spencer was a special case.

When Harry came into the diner that Friday night, hours after he'd found out, I could see the .38 he carried in his coat pocket. When you're dead, you can sense those sorts of things. I could see that he'd been crying, and he'd done his best to not show it.

He ordered his food, and his drink, and he sat at the counter, and he didn't look up. I'd known Harry now for ten years. He considered us good friends, and he often why he never took my invitation to come home and meet his family. "Work," I told him.

No matter how bad something hits an American man, he does his best not to show it. But Harry was tired, and he showed me the gun.

It was the .38 nightmen carried at the bank.

When a man confesses he's going to kill himself —or at least thinking about it —you never quite know how to handle things at first. One of the regulations about my position —about being able to physically manifest —is that, under your watch, and by your hand, no one can die from self-intention. If someone tells you he wants to kill himself, it's on your head. You don't want to break the rules.

When I left to go fight, I left my pregnant wife. I did the honorable, noble thing by serving my country –and that is an honorable, noble thing. But abandoning your wife, so to speak, is not. It's a double-edged sword. Maybe it made me a bad husband, and maybe it made me a bad father. I'll never know, now.

And I wouldn't let Harry do that, be a bad father or a bad husband, especially if he could have avoided it. He had his daughters, and his wife. He sat there, at the counter, his hair muffed and fingers shaking, with all the physical traits of a drunk but the emotional distress of a sober man. He shouldn't have let his kid go, straight from high school into the Army. Jack was only seventeen, and had begged Harry for weeks to sign the papers, to let him go in. And finally, Harry relented. And now he told me how much he regretted it.

"He would have gone anyways, when he was old enough," I said. He nodded silently. I'm not sure how much that comforted him, but it was true, and he must have realized it.

Marissa brought out our food at the same time, and she smiled politely, and kindly at Harry, who simply looked down at his plate. We ate in silence. I suppose Gary and Marissa both knew something was up, because they didn't come out like normal.

We sat quietly after we had eaten too. He pulled the gun out from his jacket pocket, quite suddenly, and held it between both of his hands. His eyes traced the barrel, and the cylinder, and the grip;

and his thumb played about the hammer and the trigger. He laid it up on the counter, and told me he still intended to go through with it, and that I had been a good friend to try to stop him.

"And what will your wife do?" I asked.

He didn't answer, just kept looking at the gun. When you're dead, you also know about life. Harry's wife was pregnant with another son, but neither of them knew it yet.

"You'll never have another son," I said as I stood, and tears began trickling down his face. "You'll never have love again if you put it all out of your life." I probably shouldn't have done it, and I knew I was risking my existence by turning my back on him and going to the restrooms, but I did. I held my breath the whole time, and when I came back out, I smiled and nodded.

The revolver was on the counter, and Harry had gone home.

God is both loving and merciful. His ways are hard to understand, unless you have the option of looking back at them to see how everything worked out. Harry was alright after that night. I went to his son's funeral, and his wife found out they were pregnant a few weeks later.

God is both loving and merciful, because he gave me a second chance at fatherhood. Harry Spencer was a special case, you see, because Harry Spencer is my son.

THE GENERAL STORE

The store sat as it always had, just outside the little country town; but now it sat quiet, and gracefully aged, and dusty. The grayed, weatherworn porch and the darkened, closed windows stared out at him in the summer twilight; the roadside, wet from the recent shower, glittered in the waning sunlight. The trees were deep green and full; and a robin sat resting on the porch railing. It was, in every respect, a beautiful upstate evening, with the city and the lights of Times Square hours behind him.

At eighteen, he'd left the farm for Harvard, had gone to work in New York at twenty-two, and now, at fifty, was without a job. He'd scaled the ladder at the loan institution, from a low-level accountant to upper management, and he'd gotten married along the way. Both of his kids were in high school now, and had their sights set on expensive schools, and expensive educations. And then came the meltdown of three years before. Overnight, the company filed for bankruptcy, and competitors picked it apart. His savings were minimal, and with his pension about to expire, they couldn't stay in New York any longer.

Between the farm and the city, he'd stopped attending church, stopped praying, even; always looking ahead, he was always declaring to himself that he didn't need God's help to make a buck. And here, standing in the shadow of his great grandfather's general store, he couldn't bring himself to ask God for help now. It wasn't that he didn't want to. It was that he realized he wasn't worthy of such a request, the way he'd lived, the way he'd ignored now the things he wished he hadn't. The long hours and the missed basketball games, and birthdays, and dinners with his wife. His kids had school plays, and he was playing for stock. All the while he told himself that his financial success would mean his family would have everything he never did, and now, he had nothing. Now, even his family had nothing.

He had failed them all. He had failed himself.

They were worried, of course. It was only natural that they would be worried. Where would they live? How would they eat? How would his children get to college, now?

The truth was, he wasn't alone. The financial rupture had ended the careers and lives of thousands. The reverberations had been felt across the country. Millions lost their jobs and their homes, and their lives. Talking heads and politicians said that the

United States was in recovery now, but recovery meant nothing to those without work.

Standing before the general store, before his own human history, he knew he'd been humbled. Not necessarily by God, but humbled simply by overreach. Or, he wondered –had God humbled him after all?

The sweet smell of lilac and honeysuckle, growing wild about the side of the building, was gentle and reassuring on the evening breeze. The leaves on the trees whispered as the wind drifted through them, and the grass, tall and green, bowed and returned upright, to bow once more in the summer air.

He closed his eyes, a hammer and the keys to the store in his hand, and suddenly, he was six again, and he could see himself helping his grandmother – his great grandfather's daughter, who took over the store with her husband –planting the seeds for honeysuckle and lilac in the garden beside the store. He'd helped her plant them.

Turning around, he saw the dirt parking lot, where once stood two self-serve gasoline pumps. There were always cars parked there, always people coming and going. There were farmers in dirty overalls; there were housewives with grocery lists; there were children, eager to see the shelves of candy inside. There were mechanics, who came in to get a handful of screws, or some oil; there were whole families, too, who came in for ice cream after a sweltering day working together in the field. The greatness and the beauty of America glowed in their eyes.

America could retain its preeminent position in the world, if it wanted to. And Brian Connelly, IV, standing before his great grandfather's general store with keys and hammer, could do the same. It was a dream he'd had, that brought him to stand before the store.

He'd dreamed of his great grandfather, had remembered the story his father told, that his great grandfather had once been paid in gold coins from a farmer who lived far, far out in the countryside. The farmer had made it rich out west, and simply brought home his wealth and farmed. His great grandfather had hidden the gold coins in the store, somewhere; and he figured he would keep them stashed away, for his family, for his descendants, for the future security of his family.

And Brian, in his dream, had discovered the coins, hidden beneath the floorboards beneath the bed where his great grandparents slept, until they could afford their own home. They'd lived for twelve years over the general store, before buying a farm and a house half a mile away. From there, his great grandfather managed the store, while trusted friends worked it; and he set about the fields and crops, and earned an income from that as well as the store.

The store was handed down to his grandparents, and then to his parents –and then, full of dreams buoyed by a few dollars in their pockets, he and his siblings had all left the farm for other states, for other places, for bigger, brighter dawns. His parents still lived in the farm, still planted corn, and raised and sold cows and horses. He'd stopped by to see them, to tell them he'd be spending the night, had related his situation to them, and they'd offered him the chance to move back in. He'd thanked them, said he'd need to think about it, but didn't commit. He couldn't commit. He'd be committing in failure.

But if he could find the gold coins –hundreds of pieces, collected over the years –he could sell them, and he could find a way to invest the money, to save his family.

He unlocked the front door, and stepped inside. A beam of light fell against the wooden floor, and the smells of oil, and dust, and the faint smell of apple cider hung in the air, like a cloud. He flipped on the switch, and the lights reluctantly turned to life. The shelves were empty, the counter was clean and worn.

As he looked around, he could see how things were even forty years ago... canned food, sugar, flour, radios, toys, cooking utensils and table cloths, sewing thread and sheets of material for making clothing, curtains, reupholstering chairs... there were hammers, and tools, nails, screws, cans of oil for engines of cars and tractors and farm machinery; there were games, and beauty supplies, and rakes, and shovels, and gardening tools... in the springs, there were flowers, and seed; and in the autumn, apple pies and cider. When the store installed freezers and fridges in the back, they sold frozen dinners and frozen meats. The store remained competitive, even with superstore challengers thirty minutes away. But in the end, his parents had closed down the store in order to keep up with the farm.

He remembered how hard his family had worked to maintain the store, to keep inventory and stock, to alter prices and offer sales, and serve people on a personal level. Even his grandparents didn't begrudge the large, superstores. They knew they lost some business to them, and knew how important the stores had become. But were sorry to see personal service disappear.

Brian Connelly, IV, climbed the stairs to his great grandparent's old apartment, and unlocked the door. There were three rooms. There was a kitchen and dining room area –the table and chairs were still there, as well as an old, old refrigerator; and there were two bedrooms. A small bathroom with shower had been installed in the 1910s. He'd spent evenings there, helping his grandmother and his mother bake the apple pies. How ironic, he thought, that he would come back to a place he'd never expected to, except perhaps to tear it down..

He went into the old master bedroom, and move aside the dusty, wooden frame. He felt around, testing the floorboards, looking for a loose one –and found it. With anxious hammer in hand, he slammed the plank, cracking it; and then used the hammer claw to rip it up. He tossed aside the pieces, and ripped up the next plank just as he had in his dream.

And all he found was debris. Wood scraps. Nails. More than likely the remains of a quick remodeling.

He fell backward, crestfallen, catching himself with his hands. His fingers went up to his face in exasperation, in horror, and he suddenly felt like crying. *There was nothing there. His life was finished. Everything was gone.*

"Son?"

Startled, he turned to find his father, standing in the doorway, worry written across his brow. He came into the room, and saw his son's face —streaked with dirt and confusion and fear —and he sat down a little stiffly at the old table.

"There's nothing there, Dad..."

"I know, son."

He looked up at his father. "There isn't anything there... I thought..."

"I know."

Golden sunlight filtered into the room through the window over the metal sink. Dust particles wandered about the air, sparkling in the sunlight, suspended as if by time itself.

"What happened to it?"

"I don't know, son," said the father, gently. His wrinkled hands folded, and hung between his knees. His gray hair, thin on his head, was a little disheveled from the light breeze outside. "It's possible the gold may never have been there at all. Maybe it was only a family legend."

Brian got up, and sat down at the table, beside his father.

"I just thought that... if I had that gold... if I had some sort of security... if there was something to put my feet on... something to stand on..."

"That's what God and family are for. We live in the world that is left for us, by the people who lived before us. And we do our best to leave it better than we found it. That doesn't mean there isn't failure, or times of trial. What matters is what you do with those tests. As long as you don't stop trying, you can't fail."

"I'm sorry I never came back," said Brian, quickly. "I left, and I went away."

"You had your life to live," said his father. "Your mother and I want you and your family to come and live with us until you get everything in order. Maybe it'll be a week. Maybe it'll be a few years. Who knows? You didn't really need that gold, after all."

"I could reopen this store," said Brian in a sudden flurry of thought. "I could manage it, and make it competitive, and expand it..."

"It is yours to do with as you wish," said his father. "Now come, let's get home before your mother worries."

"Alright, Dad. I'll be down. I'm just going to put the boards back." He nodded to his father, and then turned to replace the boards. Picking up his cell phone, he called his wife, to tell her he was figuring things out, that he would be home the next day. And he told her he loved her.

He hammered the planks secure, doing his best to keep together the splintered board. Maybe nothing was there, after all, he thought. Maybe there never was.

As he walked outside, he saw his father waiting up against the hood of his car, surrounded by the quiet ghosts of kind memories, which seemed more real now than the small tin of gold, dislodged by replacing the floorboards, and unknown to either father or son.

After all, reasoned Brian Connelly I and his wife, Mary, when they had put the gold beneath the floorboard in the first place –it would be for someone who really did need it.

THE BENCH AT FIFTH

She had sat on the bench for the past year, and he was in love with her.

He walked past her, every day, on the way to work. She was always out there, at the little park just past Fifth, just outside Central, so long as the weather was good. He had first seen her the previous spring, sitting out on the little bench every so often, and sometimes she had a cup of coffee with her; and sometimes she didn't; but she always had a book, and a backpack. Once, he had seen her in a university sweater, and that was how he knew she was in college —that same college he himself had graduated from four years before.

Her cell phone always sat on her lap, quiet, probably turned off so she could study. Sometimes she smiled. She sat on the half of the bench under the shadow of the maple behind it in hot weather; and in cold weather, she sat in the sunlight on the other side. But she always sat at the bench.

In the summer, her clothes were short and light; and in the winter, she bundled up. And she was beautiful in all seasons.

Now it was autumn, and just chilly enough so that she wore a thin scarf, the color a shade darker than the red leaves above her, and that fell around her. Her hair cascaded around her shoulders, and she sat with legs crossed, back against the bench, head tilted elegantly down toward the book she read today.

He had often thought about stopping to speak with her, but the way her hair framed her face, and the way the colors of the autumn moved around her against the gray skyline of the city, he didn't want to disturb her, to startle her out of the small Heaven in which she existed.

Every morning, on the way to the office, on the way to the graphic design studio —for that was his trade, humble though it might be —he considered stopping to speak to her, to say just a few words, to wish her a simple good morning. And he might see the title of the book she was reading, and might offer a few words about it. And perhaps it would lead to conversation, to coffee, and he would have to make an excuse for being late for work, but it wouldn't matter. At least, not to him.

But what, he wondered —what if his hello would be misconstrued? What if she thought it a nuisance? What if she stopped reading at the little park? Or worse, yet –what if she had somebody else?

Each morning, as he left his small apartment, he would resolve to speak to her. And by the time he made it to the park, for the walk to the office was only two blocks –and the little park in between both –he imagined that she would be happier not talking to him.

One Friday morning in late October, he found himself heading toward the park again, and as he rounded the block and went through the little park, there she was, bathed in sunlight, as though she was somehow eternal in that place. She was beautiful, and it was autumn.

The wind drifted through the buildings, and across the lawns and the sidewalks, and through the trees, and she sat on her bench, quiet, contemplative, beautiful.

There was nothing special about that day. He had no expensive account to handle. He had only a few dollars in his wallet. The sunlight was warm against his back, and he thought of God as the wind wound around him. But he entered the park, and he breathed in deeply; his hands trembled, and his knees were weak. But he made his way over to the bench, to the girl, her eyes cast down at her book.

And as he approached, she looked up with bright eyes and kindness.

"Good morning," he said.

"Good morning," she said.

They married three years later, in the little park by the bench in a small ceremony, watched by their families and presided over by a Father of the Church, and they left the city.

The sleepy suburbs were green, and quiet, and delicate in the summer evening. They sat on their front porch of their first home, sipping cold tea, and resting in one another's arms. They had been there a week, and they'd already been invited to dinner by their neighbors, and to parties, and they still had so much unpacking to do.

The train would take him into the city in the mornings, and bring him back to the suburbs in the afternoons, and he would spend his evenings with her.

And this, their first Friday evening, he spoke about the bench and Fifth. "I miss seeing you at that bench," he confessed; "but it's better to come home to your arms."

"They're happy to have you in them," she said, kissing his shoulder.

They sat in quiet a moment, their fingers entwined and her head against him.

"You know," she said, "I've told you before, but I'll tell you once more. I was hoping, one day, that you might stop and say hello.

"And one morning, you did."

She raised herself just slightly, so that she could look into his eyes, so he could understand just what it was she was about to tell him.

"And there was something else," she said. "Something else about that morning that was important."

"What was that?" he asked.

"It was a difficult time in my life. You remember. My grandparents dying, my mother dying, and you know I did things of which I am not proud... things most college kids do.

"But what I never told you," she said, squeezing his hands firmly, "was that I was going to kill myself that day you stopped to talk to me. I would have done it that night. I was looking for a reason to live, something, anything that meant something. I thought God hated me. And you simply walked into my life. There was the autumn wind, and then there was you."

He kissed her forehead, and he brought her back against him. "It doesn't matter now," he said. "You're here. And we have each other."

"Yes," she said. "Thank you."

He kissed her head once more, and smiled. "We should go in. We have much more to do before everyone arrives for dinner tomorrow."

"Alright," she said. "But let's just stay here, just a moment longer. When I sat on that bench, this is what I saw.

"This is what I dreamed of."

TAURUS-54

"It's exciting," said Mrs. Farley as she and her husband sat down on the couch before the digital hologram television. "Did you ever imagine in our lifetimes we'd see a manned spaceflight to Taurus-54?"

Mr. Farley leaned back in the couch, drawing his wife of ten years closer to him. "It is a marvel of American engineering," he said. He then turned his head slightly behind him, toward the stairs in the living room. "Kids!" he yelled. "Hurry up! The report is coming soon!"

At this, three children came bounding down the stairs: First there was Tommy, the eldest at age eight; then, there was Tara, at age seven; and then there was Sam, age five. Tommy had in hand his game projector, set to pause, and he settled it on the coffee table. He pressed play, and the coffee table became a miniature battlefield, with bases, soldiers, hovertanks and stealth fighters at war with an enemy encampment near Mr. Farley's coffee cup. Tommy directed a battalion of mobile infantry around the print edition of *National Review* to strike the encampment on the exposed left —"Like Stonewall Jackson," he explained.

"What do you think?" Mrs. Farley asked her children as she leaned forward. "Do you think they'll find anything? They've been studying Taurus-54 since 2054."

Sam, ever optimistic, nodded. "They *have* to find something on *this* planet," he said. "They've been looking for *years!*"

Tara nodded. "It would be nice," she conceded, "to discover that there will be something *else* out there. Some more people to talk to."

"What if they *aren't* people?" Sam said, his eyes wide. "What if they're brute *animals* and have *no* intelligence about them?"

Tara shook her head. "If God was going to create other people, surely they would be intelligent." She turned off her electronic reader.

"I don't believe they'll find a thing," said Tommy, now pessimistic after years of failed attempts to find life on another planet. "They'll run into God first."

At this, the attack on the left flank of the encampment was launched. The defenders recovered quickly though, and rallied on a ridge south of Mrs. Farley's notepad.

The phone rang, and Mr. Farley raised the universal remote to mute the hologram television and answer the call. It was Grandma Farley.

"Dears," she said over the house central speaker system. "Are you all watching?"

"We're watching," said Mrs. Farley.

"Hello Gramma!" yelled Sam.

"Hello, Sam!" said Grandma Farley. "What do you think? Will the Copernicus Superflight find anything?"

"Yes!" Sam exclaimed.

"Tara agrees," Mrs. Farley said with a smile as her daughter carefully considered a projected a map of the Taurus solar system on the living room wall.

Grandma Farley laughed. "But somehow I doubt our reigning skeptic agrees?"

Tommy paused his game. "Yes," he conceded. "Just because the planet is in a habitable zone, doesn't mean there will be any sort of life there."

Grandma Farley laughed again. "In all sincerity," she said, "do you believe that Carl Sagan was right, that our planet is only one small blue dot out of many? Or do you think that Gonzales and Richards are right, that our planet is privileged?"

"To be honest," Tommy opined in a very bored and mock-refined manner, "I'm *tired* of the whole debate. We get all worked up with *every* planet, and then we get *let down*."

"I understand," said Grandma Farley. "It would be exciting to find another race, somewhere out there in the void."

Tommy nodded. "Nothing exciting like that will *ever* happen."

"Well," Grandma Farley comforted him. "We'll just have to find out. I'm off to watch the news and see."

"We'll call you after the report, Mom," said Mr. Farley. "We all love you. We'll see you for dinner tomorrow."

"Yes!" Tara yelled, her gaze now pulled from the galaxies of light flung across the darkened wall like paint . "Dinner!"

"It'll be wonderful! I love you all, too," said Grandma Farley, and she ended her call.

Mr. Farley returned the volume to the television. A commercial for that year's Ford, the 2112 Washington Shooting Star, was leading up to the news. The car, like all other cars, could cruise along the roads on wheels, or hover up to twenty feet over the roads wherever states allowed.

The news began. Legislation was pending in Congress that would allow auto manufacturers to produce cars that could reach as much as fifty feet in the air, though the areas these cars could venture into would have to be limited. For instance, no one could fly a car into an airport, else it might get into an accident with a Superair Propulsion Orbiter Jet – which were now being produced by Northrup-Grumman for both civilian and military use. A major assault had been launched by the U.S. Marines on the shore of Antarctica to remove a terrorist operation aimed at destabilizing South America through a series of shoe-size nuclear bombs.

As usual, the reporters and producers wanted to hold their audience as long as possible for ratings. The segment about Taurus-54 at long last arrived. Tommy paused his military game, while Tara snuggled up in her mother's arm. Sam sat Indian-style, leaning against the coffee table, transfixed by the three-dimensional images.

"This news," said the reporter, "has been kept secret until this moment. It has been withheld from all media, and NASA has managed to even keep it off the interexpanse until now."

"Hurry up!" Tara implored then reporter, though she knew the reporter could not hear her.

"The American Space Superflight, Copernicus Excellence 2, has this morning reached the planet Taurus-54 on schedule and in top shape, as was expected. Captain Jenna Smith and her crew are well, and send their warmest regards," the reporter went on.

"Oh, for goodness sakes," said Sam. "Spit it out!"

"Captain Smith spoke to us by satellite just a few moments ago. We are now broadcasting the following announcement for the eyes of the American nation, and the world."

The image transformed into Captain Smith, a beautiful woman of thirty who held three degrees in aerospace engineering, astronomy, and biochemistry. "We have nothing to report," she said with a hint of disappointment in her voice. "Taurus-54 is devoid of all life, even the simplest."

The television transitioned back to the reporter, but no one was listening. Sam looked quite crestfallen; Tara shook her head. A single tear rolled down her cheek. Tommy sighed audibly, and returned to his tanks and infantry.

"They're never going to find anything," he muttered.

Mr. Farley leaned forward, his elbows resting on his knees. "Children," he said consolingly. "You know I flew shuttle missions years ago."

"And you didn't find anything, either," Tommy said resignedly as he paused his game to look at his father.

"Not quite," said Mr. Farley.

Three small faces turned to Mr. Farley like light.

"Did you find other life?" Tara asked, hopefully.

"No," said Mr. Farley gently. "I found out something much more important. You see, kids, every time we get to another planet, and find nothing, it underlies an even deeper quest. We can spend our lives searching for something, only to discover we've been searching for nothing else all along. We can seek out the farthest star clusters and the most distant planets to seek truth, only to discover we've had the truth in our hearts all this time. And so maybe, perhaps we discover that we are alone. Perhaps we're only one little speck in all of this space, but we're a privileged speck. Perhaps our world has been designed for us."

Mr. Farley looked up at the crucifix over the front door. "Maybe," he said reflectively, "maybe we really are alone in the universe. Yet, if we are, it proves in the end that we are not."

OF GOD AND YEATS

One afternoon, an old, retired man of great learning went strolling through the local mountain park with a volume of Yeats, his favorite poet. At the crest of the mountain, the old man was surprised to chance upon a young man, who was presumably speaking to the air in sad intonations.

"What is the matter?" the old man inquired of the younger.

"Life is full of matters," the young man replied.

The old man held up the volume he carried with him gently. "Reading Yeats always comforts me, apart from his religiousness."

The young man nodded kindly. "Speaking to God comforts me."

The old man drew back defensively in reproach. "Young man, there is no God."

The young man shook his head. "Sir, there is no Yeats."

The old man held up the dusty volume. "Here is proof Yeats once existed."

The young man opened up his arms up toward the earth and the universe, and then tapped the edge of the dusty volume gently. "Here is all proof *He* exists now."

Back then, every neighborhood in New York outside Manhattan had some kind of gang, some kind of local vigilante group, some kind of mob —local law and order. In Brooklyn, it was no different. I was eleven when I was hurrying home from a buddy's house, the night dark, and the shadows at my feet. You had no reason to fear those shadows in our neighborhood, because you knew that Jack Hayden and his men watched the streets, and they looked out for us. The only thing I had to fear was getting home late, and getting grounded for it. Jack Hayden, we knew, wasn't scared of anything, but if he had had my mother for a mother, who worked two shifts at the hospital and still made dinner for me and my father, Jack Hayden would be terrified of getting home late, too —not out of fear of punishment, but of making her worry unnecessarily.

That night, my feet flew across the sidewalk, still hot from the afternoon sun. The buildings and the street signs, the cars and the fire hydrants, the windows and the lampposts were a blur past me, emerging and then disappearing into the shadows again. In the fire escapes, women hung the laundry across the lines between the buildings; and fathers sat up, reading the papers, or listening to the reporters on television, the sounds of the news broadcasts drifting out across the quiet streets.

Somewhere in the distance, there were sirens, but that wasn't unusual. What was unusual was that Jack Hayden was outside that night, his slim but combative form, impeccably turned out in a tailored gray suit, beneath the harsh glow of a streetlight. He was in his forties, and it was rumored he had killed a man with his bare hands once —and we knew that he and his boys had personally beaten rival gang members into bloody pulps for trying to bring drugs into our neighborhood. They were doing a better job of it than the police, and so we respected them for keeping our streets clean, and the kids out of the gutters. And I, and all of my friends, wanted to be just like Jack Hayden, and run these streets for him when we got old enough.

But the night of June 12, 1960, was unlike any other night I could remember. As I turned the corner to my apartment building, that was when I saw Jack Hayden beneath the harsh glare of the lamp lights, several of his men standing respectfully, but protectively, at a nearby distance. And there, next to Jack Hayden, was Pete Murray, the brilliant seventeen year-old son of a dead member of Jack Hayden's group. Jack Hayden took off his hat, and his hair spilled across his forehead, his eyes dark shadows beneath the harsh glow of the lamplight.

Pete Murray was someone my older brother hung out with on a regular basis. Pete Murray managed to get straight As in school, and still hold his own on the street. Pete Murray wanted in with Jack Hayden, to avenge his father's death, and Jack Hayden had set Murray up with a job in the bar that they ran, just to keep him occupied. In the neighborhood, there was nothing more revered or esteemed than protecting our own streets. Most kids, we knew, would end up connected in Jack Hayden's circle, one way or another. If you weren't tough, and didn't actively seek to be a part of that circle, directly or indirectly –and it didn't matter if you were rejected, but only that you tried –you were shunned and shut out, a pariah. Pete Murray didn't just not want to be an outcast, he wanted blood.

I wasn't sure how the conversation had started, or how it had ended up being out there on the street corner. But I only caught the tail end of it, standing just outside the cold, metal door on the stoop of the building where I lived.

"What you mean," Pete Murray said, "is that you want me to run away. If I run away, they'll call me a coward. And I'll never be able to show my face here again."

67

Jack Hayden didn't miss a beat. "And that's a good thing, kid," he said. "Here, some of them will call you a coward, sure. They'll call you a coward for getting out, yes. But everywhere else, they'll call you a hero for rising above it all. But the ones who call you coward are the real cowards, for not having the conviction to stand up, and the courage to walk away from something that's already dead and gone and buried.

"Times will change, kid. And we won't always be here. I do this because it's what I've always done. But you have a choice, here. And you have a choice that you shouldn't waste. Right now, some goon out there is probably painting my name on the bullets he's loading into his gun. And chances are, that's how I'll die. But not you. Your father did what he had to do to get you out of here. And that's what you need to do. Go to college, get out of here, get married. Make something *real* out of your life. Or God help me, you'll be hearing from me. Because at the end of the day, you aren't a coward. And you and I both know that."

For some reason, the church bells from Saint Francis rang then —to this day, I don't know why —but it was nearly ten at night on June 12, 1960, right as they were speaking. Pete Murray got himself out of Brooklyn, went to medical school, and came back a doctor to New York. In one of those tragic twists in life, Jack Hayden, riddled with bullets, ended up on Pete Murray's operating table at the hospital ten years later. But Jack Hayden was beyond saving. Murray couldn't do for Jack Hayden what Jack Hayden had done for him. I was in training in accounting at that hospital when Jack Hayden died.

For some reason, I think God Himself may have had those church bells rung for the end of Pete Murray's former life –and mine. Because I took Jack Hayden's advice to heart that night, and devoted the next few years of my life to getting out of that neighborhood. And I did. And to this day, I can still see Jack Hayden, his tailored gray suit, his slim frame, ignited beneath the harsh light from the lamppost. He put his hat back on, and his face was a shadow, and he disappeared into the darkness –and his life eventually became a memory in our minds, dimmer with time, a shadow against the folds of eternity, like the shadows on the streets of Brooklyn.

THE HOSPITAL AND THE DINER

The happiness of others is sometimes more important than our own.

I'm not exactly sure why she decided to sit down across from me, in that dark little corner of the diner with the snug booth where I sat sipping on hot tea. But she sat there anyways; the dim lights of the diner gave the chrome-decorated place its 1950s flavor. I enjoyed it, because it reminded me of better times. Lately, I'd been there alone. But tonight was different because of the girl that sat across from me.

She was twenty-two, and fresh out of college. She said she was on her way to the hospital across the street, but she didn't say why at first. I was still wondering why she had decided to sit across from me. I massaged my wrinkled hands; they hurt so much sometimes. Maybe it was because I appeared almost grandfatherly to her that compelled her to sit there. I hadn't expected anyone to sit across from me. It was one of the reasons why I preferred the dark little corner booth.

She peered at me, perhaps trying to see my face. She told me she didn't know why she'd sat down there, but upon contemplation, understood her compellation to be the cause of some kind of trusting feeling I gave off; it was more than likely my grandfatherly appearance. I sipped my tea; the cars outside hummed past. They were predicting snow, so everyone was busy, scurrying about, gathering last minute provisions to hole up with and brace against the storm.

Her name, she told me, was Melissa. She had graduated from college the previous year, where she had studied business management. But she was still looking for a business to manage. It had been a difficult year, she had informed me. Apart from the recession, she added. She twirled a lock of her sepia hair, nervously, around her index finger. It was as though she were suddenly unsure of herself. But I motioned for her to continue. How could I not?

A waitress came up to our table, and offered to take her order. Melissa smiled weakly and asked for coffee. The waitress nodded, and disappeared behind us to greet an arriving family. The father dusted snow off of the coats of his children, and off the shoulders of his wife. The waitress showed them to a table, handed them menus, and went to get coffee for Melissa.

My young companion commented casually about how cold it had been, and about how it seemed too early to be getting snow. She didn't know why, but said that I was easy to talk to. I smiled and nodded, but I doubt she could see it in the darkened corner of the diner. I didn't mind it, though. I don't think she minded the darkened corner either, otherwise, she wouldn't have bothered to sit there. Behind the counter, two more waitresses replaced jack-o'-lanterns with pilgrims and ships.

I could tell she was upset. It is that look of all womanhood, when the weight of the world bears against them, but strong and resilient, they try to hold their heads up high, and they clean away ruined mascara simply to replace it. Soft and beautiful, she sat there; confused and hesitant, she remained.

The waitress arrived a moment later with her coffee; Melissa accepted it and said thank you; the waitress left us. And Melissa sat there, hands wrapped around the warm mug, and breathed in heavily. Perhaps the smell of coffee comforted her. Perhaps she was realizing again the weight of that worldwide burden. Perhaps she just wanted to steady herself with the quietness of a peaceful moment set against the whirlwind of snow and chaos that transpired around the silent little diner.

Or perhaps it was the recognition of something horrible.

And she told me she was on the way to the hospital across the street to see her boyfriend, William Madison. But she had to work up the courage to go and see him first, which was why she had come into the diner. And she had found my little corner.

William Madison was her age, but older by a month. They had met their freshmen year in college, at the aquarium at the harbor. Baltimore has its own quiet corners. They had hit it off. They had been all over the city, and had been all over the country on holidays. They were from middle-class suburbs somewhere out in the state. They had big plans, and big dreams. All kids do. But somehow, dreams are put to sleep after thirty. But she hadn't been sure that William would live to see thirty just a few months ago.

William had been in an accident after graduating from college. He had worked as an electrician, installing and repairing lines across the city for a larger company. They had sent him and a crew to an old building, insulated with hay, and being rehabbed, but the faulty lines had short-circuited and caught fire in the walls. William didn't make it out and had received severe burns almost over his entire body. They thought he would die, but he made it.

And Melissa had been there with him, every step of the way, through every surgery, through every therapy, through every hour of every day. But she was, understandably, tired. It had been months. And William was improving everyday. He would have scars, and damaged skin, but surgery had managed to correct a lot of problems. He had been walking, and breathing steadier. The surgery had reconstructed his face well; he looked a little different, though, or so the surgeons had told her. She wouldn't see how until tonight, now that the bandages were to be removed.

And now, she told me, he was set to be released the next day from the hospital, just across the street.

He was waiting for her, she said.

So why, I wondered aloud, was she afraid to go and see him if she had been there through every hour and every day, right there, right there alongside of him? I couldn't imagine anyone being any more grateful than he.

Because –she revealed to me quite simply –she had been unfaithful.

She looked away from me. I was not quite sure how to respond at first; her confession had caught me off-guard. There was a tense silence that followed which neither one of us seemed to want to intrude upon. Nothing is ever good enough to be true. It was a jarring reality. She twirled around her finger another lock of hair.

She wasn't sure how he would react. Somewhere along the long nights and difficult hours, she had lost herself to her pain. Her feelings had changed for others, although her feelings for him were the same; but somehow, those feelings were also different. It was more than likely partly because of the facial disfigurement, she told me. And the overwhelming burden of handling the whole situation. William had no family close-by. They could still start a family of their own... and her dreams again resurfaced.

But, I said, he seemed as though he was quite committed to her. She nodded, and wiped a tear away from her eye. That was the worst part, she explained. She wanted him to be happy. But she didn't want to be with him anymore.

But he would want her to be happy as well, I declared. I liked to think I knew something about love by now. Sometimes the happiness of others is more important than our own. Sometimes it is not.

She looked down at the table, and closed her hands around one another. I told her that perhaps she should gather herself and think about things before she visited William, before he was released the following morning. She needed to compose her thoughts, gather her feelings... There was much to think about. But perhaps it was best to begin anew tonight.

She nodded, and smiled weakly. She still wanted to see him, even if she didn't want to be with him anymore. But I told her, perhaps, it might be best to phone and inform him that she couldn't make it that night. It would better brace him for the revelation. Perhaps she understood. I told her I would take care of her coffee. She smiled again, weakly, said thank you, and stood up to leave.

The door creaked open, the wind howled, and Melissa disappeared. But William wouldn't be there to call, or to see in the morning at the hospital. She wouldn't know what he would look like after the surgery. I coughed and breathed in deeply as I watched the snow continue to fall. The waitress handed me a receipt for the tea and the coffee. I rubbed my hands, pulled out my card, placed it alongside the receipt, and signed the paper with my name: William Madison. I had been released from the hospital across the street early.

God had saved my life in that building. Melissa had helped me keep it. And now I was giving Melissa hers back.

Sometimes, you see, the happiness of others...

THE SIGN POST

After the rainstorm, when Jeremy Turner rode to the edge of his land north of the river that went south of it, he was surprised to find a singular pole −a large branch, really −rising up out of the ground, the pointed end dug in deeply, and buffeted by a pile of fair-sized rocks and stones. Such an unnatural occurrence in so naturally occurring a place struck Jeremy Turner as wholly mysterious. Jeremy Turner's dog, Virtue, approached the post without concern, sniffing about its base, about the rocks, and then looking up to Jeremy for instructions on what next to do.

The summer wind swept up from the river water, cool and steady, bending the meadow grass and the blue wildflowers, the trees along the banks shifting in contemplation of the breath that weighed against them; and the summer wind stirred Jeremy

Turner's heart, a ghost song echoing up through the land on which he made possible his life. And the wind brought movement to the post, a small, pale sheet of paper, secured by a nail, whipped up though pinned down, and settled once more.

A note.

Jeremy Turner approached cautiously. He'd heard of such things from farmers in town, from some of his neighbors in the other direction, and south of the river. Rival land claims. The need for lawyers. Government land grabs. New laws requiring wide open land be bounded by that infernal barbed wire. It could be any of these.

But it wasn't.

"Dear neighbor," the note said, "Yesterday evening two of my calves wandered onto your property, and ate up a mess of things. Please do accept my sincerest apologies."

The note was signed, "Kid".

Jeremy Turner read the note twice. His own small herd was somewhere a mile or two back. At least ways he could see, a few adventurous calves was no reason to go to war. Not that wandering cattle was a reason anyways, at least among the people north of the river. Some folks south of the river were dead set on their property boundaries, and stood out with shotguns and revolvers to make it clear. But Jeremy Turner wasn't one of them.

He pulled out the ledger in his saddlebag, and hastily scrawled a note in return.

"Neighbor Kid," it said, "No harm done and no apologies needed." He signed the note with his own name, dismounted his horse, and pierced his response by way of the nail. He then turned the branch in the other direction. Virtue looked on.

Jeremy Turner then returned to his horse, and headed off to see about his own cattle. As he rode along, Virtue close beside him, Jeremy could ever only recall catching sight of who he supposed was Kid just once, a long ways off, back in the winter, a dark form against snow-brushed hills. It was not uncommon to have an unknown neighbor, but all the better for the introduction, now.

Riding along the edge of his land north of the river that ran south of his property the following day, Jeremy Turner was surprised to find the post facing east, toward him. Curious, and with Virtue nearby, he went back over to it to discover a new note from Kid.

"Mr. Turner," it read, "I thank you for your kindness. Be on the lookout: there is a mountain cat prowling around here. I shot at it yesterday eve, but missed. If you have chickens, watch them."

Jeremy Turner did have chickens.

He pulled out another sheet from the ledge in his saddle bag.

"Much obliged, Kid," he wrote. "I'll let you know if I see or get the demon cat." He paused, wondering what he could pass along to Kid. He reflected on the opinions in town shared at the watering troughs. He wrote, "They say next year will be especially good for corn with all the rain we've gotten this summer, but to watch out for the water rising through the fall."

He dismounted his horse and posted the note, and then turned the branch back west.

Back in the saddle, Jeremy Turner could see the endless green fields beginning to turn golden in the late summer sunlight, a vast American idea; the mountains, smoke-blue, rising to meet the star-studded empyrean reaches, God's fingerprints still visible in their midst to the eye reasonable enough to understand, both beckoned and reassured.

The wind was a ghost song that wrapped itself around home.

The next day, another note.

"Mr. Turner, I thank you for the warning on the crops. I am new to planting and relatively new to the land and was considering wheat but shall sow corn this year upon good advice. Do not worry about the demon cat; I dispatched it yesterday morning." But it looked like rain, and so Jeremy Turner did not leave a response.

The rains came again and kept men and their families indoors. Jeremy Turner set about mending shirts and cleaning his rugged little hovel that sheltered him from the rage across the plains and the drifts of winter and the wild that constantly railed against his meager architectural statement of civilization. Virtue dozed happily, grateful for the break from work in the heat.

When the sunlight and a day of cool, clear weather turned up once more, Jeremy Turner set out with Virtue to the post, and wrote: "Good work with the demon cat, but be wary. Where one disappears, another will turn up soon enough." And then, as an afterthought, he added, "How are you today?"

Jeremy Turner then set about checking on his cattle, and the little barn, and went and saw that the river was perhaps a foot higher, but still in its course. The wheat was coming in well, and the chickens went wandering obliviously about that fact, far beneath the chaff, looking for fallen grains.

It was a small, temporal claim on perpetual seasons, the fields and the crops and the little house, but it was one that worked and got by.

The next day, the post still faced west. There was no note, but it did not concern Jeremy Turner. The tasks for farmers never diminished. A few words between neighbors were often exchanged weeks apart.

But the following day, the post still faced west, but it did not exactly trouble Jeremy Turner, though it made him a bit uneasy. Neighbors did not break off conversations, rare as they were, without cause.

On the third day in the morning light, Jeremy Turner faced west with the post, his revolver loaded and his Winchester Repeater readied and Virtue understanding the tenseness of his master, ready to descend upon whatever threat might be encountered. On this third day without a note, Jeremy Turner understood that something was not right. On the frontier, a thousand things can go wrong and will mean the end of a life and range from wolves and renegade Indians and bandits and broken legs and bad food and no one will have ever known that someone existed at all in an isolated place called home against a land-ocean of hills.

And so Jeremy Turner crossed over the border at the end of his land north of the river that ran to the south, into land he had never ventured onto. The land on which he lived he had purchased when opened up ten years before. His parents and younger siblings lived on land fifteen miles east, and he got around to see them once or twice every year, and all the neighbors and little towns along the way. But here, to the west, was a place he had never before ventured. It was land not his own. Though friendly in town, neighbors respectfully did not cross over onto the land of others unless invited or with sound reason. They kept to themselves, excepting.

And Jeremy Turner, uninvited and without sound reason, felt as though an intruder, and invader, trampling onto something sacred, something holy, the dreams of someone else. The meadow flowers and the trees along the riverbank and the mountains in the distance were all at once the same and not the same to his eyes, but still, God dwelled in the land. That much was clear.

He went to the top of the closest rise, the hill against which he had glimpsed his neighbor once upon a time, and the wild grass brushed against the horse and eternity, and the land opened up into a valley, and another rise, another ghostly song. And he and Virtue set off through the valley to the next rise, and from there, he could see the small cabin, less the size of his own, tucked away against the leeward side of a golden-green hill, huddled in the quiet shade of July.

The cabin itself was dark and quiet, appeared sturdily-constructed, and Virtue found nothing at which to be alarmed. But Jeremy Turner understood that his neighbor might well be lying somewhere out among the meadows.

He knocked on the door; there was no answer. He knocked again, the rapping of his knuckles against the solid oak louder, and there was some movement within. And then, startlingly, he heard the voice of a woman call out in struggle.

"Who's there? I got a loaded shotgun, and I know how to use it."

"It's your neighbor, Jeremy Turner."

Nothing.

"We've been corresponding by post," he said.

"Come to the window to the side, but stand back."

Jeremy did as he was instructed. The dirt-smudged face of a beautiful girl appeared there, dark circles under her cerulean blue eyes that shone out from the darkness in the cabin like stars in the midnight sky.

"I'm pretty sick, Mr. Turner," she said.

"I'm looking for Kid," he said.

"You found her," she said, smiling and then coughing.

Jeremy Turner folded his arms in slight confusion.

"My father bought this land," Kid explained, her fists white as they shakingly gripped the windowsill. "And we always intended to come here and farm it, but then mama got sick, and then papa got sick, and then there was only me left and so I sold what we had and came out here."

"How long have you been sick?" Jeremy Turner asked.

"I took sick in the rain a few days back. Been trying to get back on my feet, but it's only getting worse. I haven't been out to see the cattle. Do you think they're alright?"

Jeremy Turner nodded. "I am sure they are fine," he said. "I'm going to go and get Doctor Monroe in town. I'll be back in a few hours. You need to stay off your feet until I get back."

But before Kid could protest, Jeremy Turner told Virtue to remain; and then Jeremy Turner was a cloud of dust across the land, returning hours later, as promised, with Doctor Monroe. Confident that Doctor Monroe had things in hand, Jeremy Turner went home.

Sitting out on Jeremy's porch a short while later, Doctor Monroe explained that he was quite amazed at the girl's resilience, and was amazed that she had managed to survive something that should have killed her. He left it at a combination of God's grace and Kid's will, and Jeremy Turner agreed.

"She'll be alright in a few days," Monroe said. "I take it you were planning to keep an eye on her cattle?"

"Yes, sir. I planned on it."

"You need anything else, you come and get me. Keep an eye on her place, too. She'll be alright, but a girl out there alone like that? It worries me."

"I'll do just that."

"Good day and God bless, Jeremy."

"Safe trip home, Doctor Monroe. Godspeed to you."

Three days passed, and as he had for the previous two days, Jeremy Turner set out to watch Kid's cattle and to check on her cabin and to dream in the broad summer sunlight. They were amaranthine dreams of American ideas.

But at the edge of his land north of the river that went south of it, against the soft, summer breeze that whispered up from the water, a ghost song of promises, the post –the large branch, pointed end dug in deeply, buffeted by stones, faced east once more. And Jeremy Turner smiled while Virtue waited patiently.

"Dear Mr. Turner," the note read, "I wish to thank you for your kindness and your compassion these past few days. I am fully recovered and I wish to make you dinner tonight, at six o'clock. Please do come. Please bring Virtue as he is also quite welcome as well."

Jeremy Turner nodded to Virtue. "Well, boy, that certainly sounds like an invitation we can't turn down. I suppose we'd better go and dig out our better clothes and pick up some wildflowers along the way."

Just in case Kid might venture up to the post before the appointed time, Jeremy Turner left her a note.

"Dear Kid," it read, "Virtue and I thank you for your kind invitation and we'll happily be present this evening at the requested time."

As Jeremy Turner and Virtue set out across the American landscape to home, the wind swept against them, cool in the warm sun, a quiet, constant promise, a whisper of dreams.

SHOOTING STARS FOREVER FALLING UP

And so he waits upon the shore as the sun sinks west across the Chesapeake, his hands set down to touch the tide that they could never touch again, not for this century, not for a thousand years, not now, not ever, never the past, never the past returned again. The moonlight broke against the saltwater like a thousand, million stars, constellations constantly shifting, rising, falling, a mirror to the sky but a world of its own, the currant-colored water a canvas, a page ever traced by history, ever marked for one more day. The shipwrecks lay tossed about rolling hills of sand at the bottom of the Bay like forests of graves.

But here at the water's edge, he dwells in night. The sunlight speaks of everything that has gone away with the tide. But the midnight world brings back the past in life.

Not that the sunlight itself was not beautiful, not that summer azure skies and autumn-golden sunlight tracing silver paths along lilac-colored clouds, and quiet snowfall quilting the last dry island ground was not something to stir the heart, to captivate one's soul. But dreaming –remembering- was easier at night, when the darkness gave sharp relief to the past.

And memories of the past do not fade. Somewhere, some time, dreams and memories become the same thing.

Once upon a time, the young man was alive and drew breath into his soul. Once upon a time the island was a paradise, a place touched by the Hand of God and worked by the hand of man. Several dozen homes and buildings, and several dozen families and generations dwelt here on the fertile ground, rising high above the Bay, high above the tempest of the water from which most men sought a living and daily battled death. A fleet of fishers, dredgers, and crabbers swept out in the morning tides, while others took to farm fields and orchards and the thousand tiny details of everyday life. Every family cared for every family; every family was yours, too. The community grew and grew, and there was a church and a school and a post office and a doctor's residence and baseball teams and stores and fairs and weddings and births and a million golden sunrises –and all the while, the island disappeared beneath them. Here the young man made a life and married. And here the earth betrayed him. They did not know the ground was falling away beneath their feet until it was too late.

The shore crept ever closer to the homes as time and tide and storm and squall claimed one more piece of land, carried one more breath of life away. The people retreated; the water came on. The fertile earth was waterlogged; the fresh ponds all turned brackish; the old docks soon lost their hold on land, and crumbled in the waves. Roads became tidal riverbeds. One by one the families left; one by one they left their homes, though sometimes took their houses with them for the mainland. But they never took their homes.

The only thing they left of any value was their dead.

Three hundred years of dead.

Three cemeteries once stood here. Two still remain. One rests on the last remaining ridge. One rests on a small, sinking knoll in the center of the island. The last rests lost now beneath three feet of water. And the twilight starlight summons up the dead among scattered bricks and shattered glass tossed along the shorelines, among the broken pottery and hollowed-out foundations sinking in the marsh.

The young man makes his home now in the center cemetery, standing there among weatherworn marble stones and rusted iron fences around which underbrush has grown and taken hold. In the sunlight, yellow-green-and-olive saltmeadow and smooth cord grass rise up from meadows turned to marsh through which egrets call and white terns sweep and dragonflies dart like dandelion seed upon the breeze. In the present world, barely anything of all that once was here can still be found. But still he knows the places. Still he knows where things belonged. There was a farm along that solid rise, now in the last ten years the new shoreline. There, the church stood tall and bright before the sun, yet now only its cemetery and some battered, broken bricks remain. Over there was once the little village square, now a tidewater pool.

But it is in the night when things are changed and remembered. The starlight falls down upon the earth like snowfall, resurrecting phantom images of homes long gone, of land long lost, of memories unknown but to the dead. And here through these reflections, the young man races among the yards and the picket fences and the sandy roads that rolled across the land, to the places where he kissed the girl and married her, to the places he called home and the memories he called his. The dead rise up from their cemeteries in the chill of the October night, their forms like heated breath in the autumn wind. The world is transformed; and there, they traced the sacred paths they walked in life on land now resting far beneath the waves. And they remembered:

"Here I kept my garden."

"Here I kept my home."

"Here I kept the orchard."

"Here I never stood alone."

And the fluttering of the waves, and rush of wind through the few remaining cedars, and the calls of tired birds conspire in an ethereal epithet of melody, a chorus, a song, a dream by which the dear departed dead dance like the living in the night. If only to remember, if only to remember how to dream, if only to remember what it was to live. As each year passes, some of these revenant souls let go of their earthly bonds, of the ties that bind them to tideland ground, and rise up in the night to take the Hand of God, shooting stars that are forever falling up. Every year there are fewer still, as every year there is less left to the island.

But the young man still remains each year, for his wife is still alive.

He remains long after all the other souls leave. He waits for decades, one after another, through the fall of autumn leaves and the melting of the winter snows. He sees the fashions of living visitors change each year, the design and composition of their boats forever modern, forever sleeker, forever of the future. He listens to the things those people say, those of flesh and blood and air and beating hearts. Most are disappointed by the island, expecting ghosts and demons, scares and thrills, abandoned houses and spider's webs, but their eidolonnic conjurations are set to rest. Others call the island creepy, weird, or boring. Some see the island as proof that nature retakes everything man once tried to claim, such as where the underbrush grows high above the tombstones.

But the ghostly young man sees the past between the phantom ruins, sees what stood once among the marsh, a chimeric shade of everything that was. The ghostly young man knows the truth. It is not horror, but home. It is not weird, but welcome. It is not nature rising up to claim that cemetery on the little knoll as the living think, but nature growing up to protect the resting places of the dead from an encroaching ocean wilderness. At least then for that time, erosion will not steal another grave.

He waits among these island graves in the blue moonlight, traces the letters of his name in his weather-faded stone, one hundred years asleep, one hundred years alone. But there is something different now tonight.

He senses now the glowing misted shores, can smell the saltwater tides that bear upon the falling land. He can feel the wind against his skin for the first time in too long, can feel the cool, fresh take of air in lungs too long unused. And as the incandescent veil of fog is parted, sweeping down now to the sand-set earth like a valley from the mountains, she appears, an amaranthine light inside her eyes, her love, her beauty now as it was a century ago. And now, for the first time in so long, his heart begins to beat again. It races as she draws near, and storms of glittering light break apart the night like fireflies and shooting stars and up they ascend, a swirl of radiance and brilliant faith and resplendent love returned and reunited, a whirlwind dancing tide to Heaven's gates to warm their souls in the light of God. They are shooting stars forever falling up.

And far below, now alone, the island slumbers in the blackest night, the water creeping ever closer to those last few traces of the place that human beings called home. But now even their ghosts have gone away, on to better times. Still the island slumbers, sinking faster as the centuries course on. One day too, the island will be gone, submerged beneath the rolling waves of time.

And then, who will be left to remember?

But to the dead the island still remains.

GRADUATION DAY

It was as if he stood on the edge of the abyss. In reality, he simply stood on the low, foot-high fieldstone wall between the lawn and the front garden. But better that it were the abyss, for it might well have been.

The warm morning sunlight fell down against his back, and the cold, clear water poured from the emerald-green hose he held, raining down on the sepia mulch. The smell of wet earth rose among the scent of the golden marigolds beneath him; the pleasant throngs of robins and the hum of car engines circled about him through the neighborhood, and there he stood at the edge of the abyss.

He –John –looked at his watch. His youngest brother, Seth, eighteen, ten years younger than John, would be graduating from high school in two hours. At the end of the summer, it was off to California for college. The middle brother, Alex, was home from school up in Boston for the season. And John lived at the edge of the abyss.

Really, he lived in a room he rented from his parents over the garage. He had graduated when the recession had begun, was passed down for a job in New York upon graduation because the company wanted someone more experienced −even for a start-up position −and so John went home and had worked innumerable odd jobs to get by.

It was a day for dreamers. It had always been a day for dreamers, for their dreams were the interwoven threads and strands that formed the fabric of the day, a canvas just beginning to be filled in. Here was the end of the world, from which jumping, one could sail in any direction, could write their own future, and come around back only to show was had been accomplished in the time since they had gone.

John, too, had felt that way once upon a time, once upon a day for dreaming. But rather than jumping out across the abyss, he had fallen in. But it was best not to think of that. He had to remind himself, day after day, year after year, that he was simply doing what he could, that it was only a matter of time before he, too, finally jumped the gap. Time. Just time. Too much of it. And too little in a human life.

"Hello, John."

The voice, soft and graceful as the June morning sun, brought him back from the edge of the abyss.

"Good morning, Jessie." She was one of Seth's best friends and might as well have lived at the house. Her hair was auburn in the morning sun, but her eyes did not reflect the light that fell down around them like a shroud.

"I'm not bothering you, am I?"

"Not at all," he said.

She wore her graduation dress, an ultramarine blue, silk, that shimmered like mountain spring water. All he was missing was his jacket, folded across the chair of his desk in his room.

"I just wanted to walk," she confessed. "The morning was so beautiful... and so suffocating."

John's head turned slightly. "Suffocating?"

Jessie nodded, but said nothing. She appeared as though she was on the verge of tears, as though the berm that held them back was paper thin, as though the slightest provocation would break her apart like glass. Somewhere, a robin sang.

"Is it bad?" she asked, looking back at the morning streets of the neighborhood. "Is it bad out there?"

"It is tough," John said. "But it's worth it."

Jessie followed John around to the side of the house to turn off the hose. They stood there, in the cool, dew-slicked grass of the shade of a lilac tree.

Jessie folded her arms. "I suppose it's easy to dream when things are holding you back. And then when you're free to act, it's hard to dream." She looked up at his eyes. "Were you afraid?"

John nodded. "Certainly, some," he admitted.

"You've always given me good advice, John. You've always been kind and honest with me. And I know that you're not happy where you are, but it's meant a lot to me that you've been here to talk to all these years. So can you tell me something?"

"Sure."

"You know what I've done the past four years... Homecoming Queen, Prom Queen, captain of the field hockey team, captain of the lacrosse team, all AP classes this past year... I go to Church every Sunday, and I pray before I go to sleep at night, and I volunteer at the soup kitchen in town. I'm a poster child for the all-American girl." She smirked and laughed, the humor a little self-deprecating. "I mattered for those four years... But what I need to know... What I need you to tell me is, will I matter out there?"

"Of course." It was true. It was unhesitatingly said. "You will matter so long as you let yourself."

Jessie nodded, but John wasn't sure if she truly accepted what he had said.

"Do you ever feel," she wondered, tracing a circle in the dew-wet grass with her shoe, "do you ever feel like time is running out? Like things move too fast?"

Yes, John thought. All the time. It disappears as fast as the morning dew in the summer sunlight. But it was not what he said.

"You're too young to think about things like that, yet," he said tenderly. "You're a young woman, and you've got decades to worry about time. You're too young for that, now."

Jessie looked up at him, her eyes honest, her voice unhesitating. "So are you."

She looked at her phone. "I'd better head back. My grandparents are going to be here in a few minutes."

"I'll see you on the stage," John said.

"I'll look for you," she said. "Thank you for everything. For always." She kissed his cheek, her lips soft and warm, a slight trace of lipstick left in their wake that she tenderly brushed away with a thumb.

She left him standing in the quiet shade of the lilac tree. She was halfway across the lawn when she heard John's voice.

"Jessie... You'll always matter. Always, to me."

A ghostlike smile, there and not there, out like the tide before anyone was awake to notice it, and she continued the block home, out into the summer sunlight like a dream.

No, John thought. There was no end to dreaming. And it was time to go.

He watched his brother march across the stage, watched Jessie march across the stage, the crowd applauding, the families and friends cheering, the blue and white gowns swaying, the tassels turned, the caps thrown into the air, pomp and circumstance, tears of joy, tears of understanding that things would never be the same.

The streetlights came on, yellow and ethereal in the summer evening, the sun sinking in the west, and the stillness of the time made it seem as though time, for once, was suspended. And Jessie stepped along the sun-warmed sidewalk, her shadow long, and the smell of grill smoke in the air from the graduation parties in countless backyards across the town. And there would be countless more parties in the days ahead.

And she came to the house she had visited that morning, one among a hundred, where Seth and John lived. And the sounds of music, of laughter, of love, drifted over the house and out onto the street from the backyard like a spring fog across a meadow. And there, out front, was John once more, watering the marigolds that he and his mother had planted a month before. And she noticed a single piece of luggage in the back seat of his car, quiet and ominous in the darkening world.

"Are you going somewhere?" she asked as she approached him.

"I am," he said.

"When did you decide this?" she said, the suspension of time eroding. She felt as though she should have known about this before, but she could not understand why she felt she had the right to demand such things.

"About an hour ago."

She breathed in deeply the smell of clear water and moist earth. "For how long?"

"A few days," he said, and she relaxed, exhaling. "I need to do a little dreaming. To get away, I guess, for a little while."

"You'll text me, and let me know how you are?"

John nodded. "Yes."

"And you know I'll be here when you get back," she said to reassure him, and herself, "in a few days. When you get back..."

Neither one of them knew exactly what she meant, what she was saying exactly. But for then, it was enough. She stepped up beside him on the small wall above the garden, joined him up on the edge of the abyss. Her bare arm, and his forearm, touched, warm, electric, comforting.

"I should get back," she said, "before anybody misses me. But before I do... I wanted to tell you about how annoying it was, waiting for commencement outside the auditorium. So, I'm standing there with Megan and Emily, and Emily had on this *horrendous* flowery perfume, and every bee in the world decided not to leave us alone..."

Jessie's voice, soft and tender, and full of light at last, wrapped itself around both her and John, and it drifted away into the night with the fireflies. It rose far above the neighborhood, up and beyond the abyss, rising among the voices in a thousand yards, and with a thousand other dreams, touched the foot of the eternal firmament of Heaven.

THE LAST NOVEL OF ELLISTON HERBERT

Elliston Herbert was ninety-nine years old when he disappeared from wall above the seaside cliff beyond his California castle. I knew him for only one year, as his groundskeeper. There was nothing absolutely remarkable about that one year, up until the final day at least. I had started my senior year at UCLA, and needed a job to get me home to South Carolina on holidays. Elliston Herbert had taken out an ad in the Los Angeles Times for a groundskeeper, and so I applied. The pay was good. The work was tough sometimes. The experience was something I never expected.

Herbert was one of the great American writers who existed in the periphery of the national consciousness. His novels sold, but he was mostly unknown to the younger generation –to my generation –for his flourishing had been decades before. Now he was unsung. But he wrote, and he published. He'd had a couple of books turned into films, and had amassed enough money to construct a manor house of sorts, north of Los Angeles. Surrounded by walls that resembled castle fortifications out of Old Europe, the manor house was perched on the rocky shoreline of the Pacific.

His home was stately, and elegant. The manor itself was a combination of Gothic and Tudor designs; and a rose garden swept around its sides. A single road led through a gate, through the courtyard formed by the walls, and revolved in a circle before the house, before trailing around to the garage in the rear. There was little I knew about Herbert before I went to work for him. I knew who he was, but knew nothing else. I decided to pick up a recent anthology of his short stories to see what he was like in his writing, and I was pleasantly surprised by the utter gentility and quiet sophistication of his prose. Barely anyone wrote like that anymore.

He was waiting for me, on the front steps of his home, his hands folded in front of him, a cigar in his right hand. A wedding ring –the only physical trace of his late wife –was on his left hand. Except for a maid who came around every other day, he'd lived alone on the cliff north of Los Angeles for twenty years. He greeted me warmly, and took me about the property, showing me the lawns, and the fountain, and the pool, and the gardens, in which stood a small shrine to Mary, Mother of God. He showed me the view from the top of the manor house tower; and we went along the castle walls, which stood the rocky land two hundred feet above the ocean water, raging and swirling against jagged rocks below.

He also introduced me to his maid –an Eastern European girl from Albania, named Adelina. She dressed like an American college girl in every respect, but the only telling difference was her accent. She was working her way through her sophomore year, but at what college, I didn't know. Had I remembered, it wouldn't have mattered in the end. The girl was gorgeous, and she kept her hair in a loose tie at the back of her head.

Herbert was a gentleman. The hours I kept were my own. I was to be paid daily. So long as the work was finished, the hours didn't matter. That appealed directly to my class schedules. And so I worked twice as hard, keeping the gardens tidy, keeping the lawns trimmed, keeping Herbert's property as graceful as it had been when I'd arrived.

Herbert dreamed while he was awake. He went along the castle walls, alone, the dark silhouette of his form against the cerulean blue sky. The final week I knew him, Adelina was heading to leave for the afternoon, and she stopped by to say hello to me in the garden, where I was pulling the dead branches from the rose bushes.

"Have you read any of his novels?" she asked me.

By then, I had only read two, and I confessed as much. But there was a lot I'd understood in them.

She ran her hands through her hair, and adjusted the tie that held it up. I glanced up at her, radiant and beautiful in the clear, warm sunlight; and I wondered if this wasn't how Herbert must have seen much of the world. He saw the beauty in it that others missed. His ideals were from a different time, but they shone true in his words. Popular culture would have seen Adelina in purely sexual terms; Herbert, and tradition saw Adelina as something quite different. I was seeing her that way, too, I realized. There was much more beauty to her than her contemporaries would have her reduced to.

"His novels are like dreams," she said. "He explained to me once how he wrote. It was an act of love, of personal commitment. It doesn't matter whether it is fiction, or nonfiction. A writer must begin with a belief in love –the love to dream, to understand, the love to love. Anything anyone does must begin with love, with the voluntary application of human free will. Otherwise, God's gifts to us are wasted."

She turned around, looking at the walls that hid away the dry, dead hills; and she opened the palm of her hand and gestured toward the green lawn, the red roses, ponds, and the pool, and the house. "Mr. Herbert created all of this *ex nihilo*. From nothing."

As she turned to leave, she smiled at me. "He's working on his next novel," she said. "I think it's going to be his best yet." I watched her go, and then looked up at the walls above me. Herbert had gone on further down the wall, to a place where it angled to and then away from the cliff. His eyes were towards the horizon.

There was something almost magical about Herbert's home. He'd participated in every phase of the construction himself; and his home was a Heaven on earth against the harsh, yellow ochre backdrop of the sandy desert hills and rises. He had taken desert sand and created a home. And he was noticed by the California Wilderness Protection Service for it.

Herbert's family had owned the land long before he lived there. They purchased several acres for a few hundred dollars, which, in those days, was a lot of money. Back then, no one wanted the land; and no one had any use for it. The cities went up along the coast, and the houses went up along the hills, and the environmental agencies laid claim to all the land they could find. Wildfires destroyed neighborhoods and dreams, but Herbert's castle survived two such rages.

But the castle was under siege by more than just wildfires. The environmental agencies −especially the California Wilderness Protection Service −was seeking to use the courts and the gross concept of eminent domain to dislodge the novelist, to save a rare insect that burrowed in the ocean cliffs below his home. Ironically, the little bugs burrowed so many holes into the cliffs, it collapsed them and probably killed themselves more often than not. But Mr. Herbert had the rights to the cliffs around his home, and so he fought the California government in court, through legal means, every step of the way.

That battle had been going on for years. But Herbert retained his lawyer, who retained the property for him; and Herbert went on, dreaming and writing and bringing something of beauty into the world, for the few people who still desired to see it –or sought to believe in it. Every year or so a new novel came out; sometimes, they'd appear briefly on the bestsellers lists, but such an occurrence was rare. Herbert didn't care. He'd been at the tops of those lists, once. The world had changed, not him. It was up to individuals to bring the world around, and Herbert was an individual.

Over the course of the year, he gave me copies of his books, which I read and fell in love with. I looked up old reviews online, and saw the critical acclaim. On dates I had, I'd mention to girls I was working for Herbert –and more than one of them still read his novels. There really was something different, something profoundly beautiful in the things he committed to words –and in the worlds he created in the pages existing between two covers, between end and beginning. The answers, in the beauty of creation, were all there. Interpretations of those answers may have been relative, but the answers themselves were universal.

News coverage was universal when the state court ruled against Elliston Herbert –using eminent domain. He was given eviction notices. He tore them up and flung them over the wall like dust. For months the process occurred. Reporters called. His book sales went up as his image became part of popular culture. He was rediscovered, and became something of a hero to those railing against government excesses. He was maligned by environmentalists, and green movement organizations. But Herbert stayed on in his castle, atop the cliffs above the Pacific.

He was given one last eviction notice, before he would be arrested for trespassing on what was now the state's property –his own home.

The last morning I saw him, he met me on the steps of the manor, just as he had the first day one year before. The gardens were bright, and green, and flowers grew about the fieldstone walls. The sun warmed my back, and the lawn was a patchwork of sun and shadow from the trees and palms that rocked gently with the ocean breeze. The scent of lilies from the pond, along with salt water, was on the air.

He handed me four things: a key, to the file cabinets in his basement, where he stored his unpublished work; a key to his home; a letter of recommendation to be used at whatever job I sought when I graduated; and two week's notice of pay.

"It has been a pleasure," he said, "discussing God and the globe with you."

I asked him what he intended to do, where he intended to go.

"I have relatives back east," he said. "My children. I believe I'll meet up with them, perhaps, and move back to New York, where I was born. You may read anything you wish, but do please pack up my writing and send it to them. There is a written letter sitting on the first cabinet detailing how I'd like them shipped, and to whom."

I told him I would do just that.

"There is one week between my eviction, and their deconstruction," he said, with a hint of sadness in his voice. "That will be enough time for you to arrange things. You'll also notice that there is a manuscript by my desk, which I will be completing today. The address for the publisher is beside it. I will not have the time to mail it."

I told him I would do that as well.

"You've been a good friend," he told me.

Adelina drove up as he said this. "Without love in your life, there can be no beauty. Without beauty in your life, there can be no love. Without God, without freedom, there can be neither."

I didn't know what to say. Adelina came up the steps, smiling, and she and Herbert went inside. I stood there, watching them go up the steps, and then turned back to my own car. I was suddenly aware of a chill, of a coldness to the spring air, a coldness that the warmth of the sun could not hide. And I was aware that, for the last time, I was seeing the beautiful things Elliston Herbert had created, *ex nihilo*.

That evening, when I ate, I put on the news. I was horrified to see an aerial view, from a helicopter, of Herbert's home. There were a dozen police cars along the road, and a S.W.A.T. truck. There were other helicopters circling the walls. The headline at the bottom of the screen explained that famed novelist

Elliston Herbert refused to surrender his property, and was now considered a trespasser. The situation was entirely out of hand. Furthermore, it was reported that he wasn't alone. I immediately thought of Adelina; perhaps she was stuck inside, and didn't want to leave –thus meaning the gate would be opened, and then the police would move in.

But it wasn't Adelina. According to the news anchors, there were a number of people inside as well. I could see them clearly, from the footage: there was an artist, painting in the garden. There were a group of men dressed up in colonial era costumes. And there were several companies of militia, in what appeared to be American military uniforms. And among others, there was a construction crew, moving about and examining the walls. The police were calling in reinforcements.

I doubt any of them ever read Herbert's books. It was fantastical. The artist was from a contemporary novel about a painter without a patron. The colonial costumed men were the Founding Fathers, from Herbert's historical fiction novel about the Philadelphia Convention. The companies of soldiers were World War I American doughboys, from his novel about the 77th Infantry Division in the Argonne Forest. The construction crew was from his novel set in modern day New York.

The newscasters said that Herbert had probably hired actors, in a last big show. But the presence of armed men meant more units from SWAT were being called up. I had the uneasy feeling that things would somehow turn against Herbert. The newscasters suddenly got very excited, for there, along the wall in the shot, the camera now zeroed in on Herbert, walking along the parapets; and as he reached the top of a flight of steps to descend, he looked up, smiled, and waved.

I decided I would go talk to him.

I drove out to his home, racing against the evening sun, already low in the sky, treading relentlessly to the horizon. I had to pull aside a number of times for police cars and SWAT vans that careened past me, kicking up dust as they went.

By the time I got to Herbert's home, the walls were surrounded. Doughboys manned the parapets at intervals. I told the officer in charge I was a friend of Herbert's, and wanted the chance to talk to him. Perhaps I could convince him that none of this was worth it. But before the officer could respond, Adelina called out from above the gate.

"Mr. Herbert will see you," she called to me. The police outfitted me with a microphone and radio, and sent me in. The gate closed behind me, and Adelina took me up onto the walls, down the length of the cliffs. Herbert was up there, leaning against the wall, arms folded, smiling gently.

The sun-warmed stone and the glittering, pale yellow color of light that shimmered on the surface of the dark water, out to the horizon, gave the evening a mythical, dreamlike quality. The evening stars were already bright in the darkening sky.

"It's no use telling me to give myself up," said Elliston. "They're preparing to force their way in."

"Is it really worth all this?" I asked.

"To believe in the things you love, to stand for them, is a noble thing. I believe in a better world."

The old writer stood, and smiled at Adelina. She returned the smile, and they went a little ways down the wall. I stood there, unsure whether or not to follow. On the other side of the courtyard, gunfire erupted. The officer in charge told me over the radio to find safe cover. Looking back, Herbert and Adelina had gone to the angle of the wall that went to, and then away from the rocky shore. I took a step toward them, with the helicopters circling overhead, and then they stepped up onto the wall.

My heart froze.

They looked straight ahead of them, and stepped off the edge.

As they did so, the firing all around us stopped. The officer in charge confirmed there were no casualties, and the gate had been taken. The defenders had suddenly disappeared.

I rushed over to the wall, and looked down at the spires of jagged rock below. I could not see Herbert, or Adelina. They were simply gone.

I turned around, to see SWAT members moving through the courtyard, but everything was gone. The lawn, once green and lush, was dusty, dry, and overgrown. The rose bushes were dead, and the gardens had withered. The stone walls had suffered what seemed two hundred years of damage in the span of a moment. The manor house was old, and the windows were shattered, and the wood was old and weatherworn, and frayed. The people, the characters from his books, were all gone. Everything was gone.

The California State Police, and SWAT, and an army of investigators, could not understand what had happened. The aerial footage of Herbert and Adelina's plunge went viral online. I watched the clip a thousand times myself. They hit the water, and they simply disappeared. There were no splashes, no point of impact. They never found their bodies.

Herbert's last novel was published. It turned out to be a semiautobiographical novelization of his life. It was the story of a writer, who lived among his creations, and had created beautiful things from nothing. Like God, there was a light in the darkness, which the darkness did not understand. The creator became a trespasser in the name of public use. And so the creator left the world.

Herbert's wife, Amanda, had been mentioned in the reviews and biographical sketches of Herbert's life on the backs of his books. But Amanda was not her real name. It was Adelina.

When Herbert left, everything beautiful he created went with him. *Ex nihilo, ad nihilo.*

From nothing, to nothing.

THE SUNLIGHT

They had walked for hours to reach the place they wanted to camp. Moonlight poured down against the earth; and the trees shifted in the midnight breeze and glittered with the light of a thousand fireflies.

And the young man and the young woman secured their tent and went to sleep.

They slept for hours.

When they emerged from their tent, golden sunlight swept the land and the sky and the forest, casting long, soft blue shadows like ripples in a pond.

And the young man and the young woman stood there in the sunlight, his hand held tightly in hers.

"What time do you think it is?"

"I'm not sure... I don't know how long we slept. It could be early morning, it could be early evening."

"I wish we knew," the young woman said. "But I guess we'll know soon enough."

The young man kissed her forehead. "Well," he said quietly. "I suppose it really doesn't matter, does it? Whether it's morning or evening, they both mean a new day is coming."

THE TIME PAINTER

The first time I ever met the Time Painter, he was on the misty shores of Truro on the Cape, just as the sunlight burned away the fog for clear blue summer skies. He was ninety-six years old, then; but when he was a young man in his forties, his paintings of sunrise-brushed canyons and sunset-draped mountains in the Southwest had propelled him to fame because of the colors that he used –the heathered ochres and pastel roses and smoky blues – colors few others could draw from the land.

I was an art student then, and I stood there on that Truro beach with my far inferior talent and canvas turned away from the man, clutched protectively beneath my arm so that he could not see it. I stood there and watched him work, his arms rising and falling, one brush, then another, one color, then another, the conductor and his orchestra of light and color and meaning; and I saw his canvas radiate the way that existence must have at the beginning of Creation.

And then he signed it, and stepped back from his aged, battered, portable wooden easel, the painting complete, and he turned his head ever so slightly before shaking it in disgust. He took the painting, and dropped it onto the sand. He picked up his easel, and disappeared into the fog.

I stood there, stunned and disbelieving –that I had seen a man whose art inspired my own, and that he had just taken something so beautiful and simply left it there for the tide.

I approached the painting cautiously, not wanting to kick sand on the wet oils; and I knelt down and picked the painting up as though it might shatter.

"It's horrible, isn't it?"

I jumped.

The Time Painter stood behind me.

"Horrible?" I asked, thinking I had heard him incorrectly.

"*Horrible*," he repeated.

"Not at all," I said. "Why would this be horrible?"

"Because it isn't that way anymore."

I glanced from the painting toward the sky, and it was as if the two were indistinguishable from one another. One *was* the other.

"What do you mean? This is pretty much perfect..."

"Nothing is that way anymore," he said, his eyes traveling from the painting to the canvas of the sky.

"I don't quite know what you mean," I said as I turned back to him.

But the Time Painter had gone away into the fog.

I set aside my own work for the rest of the day and sought out what I could about the old artist online. There was precious little information about him, except that most of his work for the past several decades had been written off as "cheap, sentimental nostalgia", "boring", and "unreal Realism in an age of realism".

I waited for him, painting at the shore each day for the rest of the summer, and then I had to return to school.

I did not see him again until the following summer, this time on Smith Island in the Chesapeake Bay. My girlfriend and I had taken a ferry to the three little villages there for the day; and as we strode down quiet streets warm in summer sunlight, there he was on the edge of a public dock, alone, with his easel and his canvas.

And his canvas of the marshland and the Bay waters was less a painting and more a clear glass window. The light, the colors, the textures, the subject, the passion –all of it –was radiantly clear.

"That's how I want to paint one day," I told my girlfriend. She gave my hand a gentle, encouraging squeeze.

The Time Painter signed his work, and stepped back from it as he had on the Truro shore, and then shook his head.

My hands went cold as he held the painting carelessly over the edge of the dock.

But he did not drop the painting. He set it against a post, packed up his easel, and turned to find my girlfriend and I watching.

"You again," he said amiably, and then he looked at his painting. "It isn't any better."

He handed the canvas to my girlfriend. "A gift," he said.

"What do you mean this isn't any better?" my girlfriend asked. "This is *beautiful*."

"Well," said the Time Painter, now a dozen steps away from us. "It *was* beautiful."

I did not see him for another four years. He was one-hundred years old when I encountered him again on Fire Island, near Long Island.

I was there with my girlfriend-turned-wife, and our first child on vacation when, on an early morning walk, I saw him again beside the lighthouse. Employed steadily by a graphic design firm in New York, I was by then confident in my abilities, and so I had no concerns about approaching the man. Dusk was falling, and the very first stars in the very distance could be seen above the water.

Just as before, it was as if someone had simply thrown open a door, and there was the painting. Or at least, what I could see. The artist, working, obscured most of the painting.

"You seem to like the water," I said.

"You again," the Time Painter said kindly. "Yes, I suppose that's true. The water does not know the time has changed. It still remains while nothing else ever does."

I realized then what he had meant all along. "So you *aren't* painting what you *see*. You're painting what you *remember*. You're painting what *used to be*."

"When you paint, it isn't only about what you can see. It's about what can't be seen, too. And how do you convey that into a painting?"

"You mean when you capture the soul of a place," I offered.

The old artist nodded. "It depends on how much of yourself you put into what you paint. It depends on how much of yourself you put into what you write, or build, or whatever it is you do."

I watched him work a few moments longer, and then he stepped back from the painting. I expected him to do away with the canvas the way he had with the previous two that I knew of; but he didn't shake his head. And it was then that, in the painted sands on the shore of Fire Island, I saw a young woman and two small children in the glittering, sunlit surf. A happy family.

I looked at the artist, who smiled at the painting he had made; and then I glanced up at the beach, but I could see no one in the water at all.

"But this one is perfect," the Time Painter explained. "My wife and children."

I turned to speak to the artist, but he was gone. I looked in every direction around me, but I couldn't find him anywhere. I circled the lighthouse and its cottage and the boardwalks; I went out as far as the road and the Coast Guard Station; but I could not find the old artist anywhere.

I returned to his painting, still sitting on his battered old portable easel, prepared to wait for him until his return. But as I stood before the painting like a late autumn field in the sway of the evening wind, I noticed now a new figure in the painting, someone I swore had not been there before.

As I looked more closely, I realized the man in the painting was the Time Painter –younger, but definitely him –and he was running across the sand to join his family in the water.

BEAUTIFUL, THESE SUMMER NIGHTS

"That makes every night this month."

John Berman turned to his wife, Sarah, who turned back to the novel she was reading.

"That makes every night this month you've been spying on poor Fred. Don't wake up the kids. Keep your voice down and get back in bed."

"But what do you think he's *doing* out *there*?"

"You could just ask him, sweetheart."

There was no sarcasm or malice in Sarah's voice. She was genuinely making a suggestion.

"But then he'd *never* tell me," John said unhappily. He turned to his wife from the window. "Think about it... If he didn't mind people knowing what he was doing, he wouldn't be doing it in the middle of the night."

It had begun unintentionally. John had gotten up to brush his teeth that first night, had seen Fred's back porch light on, and had seen Fred standing out in the middle of the yard, his head turned toward the Heavens, toward the array of glittering stars thrown out across the night sky like snowfall that night. John thought nothing of it. After all, Fred was a retired orbital pilot, having only recently completed his last passenger shuttle trip to the American colony on Jupiter. Now, he was grounded back in suburban Tennessee, retired at the mandatory age of ninety-five. Fred had flown since he graduated college at twenty-two. Flight was his life. But since that night, every night, Fred had traversed the expanse of the lawn for the little crimson-washed shed.

"He might just like his privacy," Sarah offered, turning the page.

John remained rooted at the window. "But what's he *doing* out there?"

It was then that he noticed Rob's upstairs light on through the window. Rob lived on the other side of Fred.

The next afternoon, returning home from work, John waved to Rob. Rob set down his hedge clippers, put his hands in his pockets, and met John on the sidewalk.

"So you saw Fred, too?" John asked.

"He's been going out to that shed *every night* for a *month*," Rob said. "And I can't figure *out* what he's *up* to. Mary tells me to leave it alone and go to sleep, but the kids and I are all curious now."

"I just don't know what he's *doing* out in that shed," John lamented.

"I saw him studying a map of the stars last week," Rob revealed. "He doesn't even use a telescope to look at them."

"Just stands there with the map?"

"Just *stands* there with the map."

"Just stands there..."

"And then there's the *crate* on the other side of the shed. Have you seen *that*?"

"*No*," John said. "*No*, I *haven't*."

"It's there," Rob declared. "It's just *sitting* there."

"What on *Earth* could he possibly be *doing* out there at night?"

"*Whatever* it is, he doesn't want *anyone* to know."

"*That's* for sure."

"Probably just wants his privacy," Mary said suddenly from behind them in the driveway. "Just the way I want this yard in order for the barbeque tomorrow afternoon."

"We're considering old Fred," Rob explained.

"I'm considering hiring a gardener," Mary countered.

Rob considered this, then addressed John. "We'll try to find out from good old Fred Saturday when he's at the barbeque."

"Sounds alright to me. But we've got to do it so we're not asking. We'll have to coax it out of him."

"Right. We can't just ask a man his business."

"Right."

John retreated home. Sarah kissed him and took his briefcase as he stepped inside.

"I saw you talking to Rob. Mary says Rob has been maintaining a nightly vigil, too... You *could* just *ask* Fred," Sarah said kindly.

"What kind of man asks another man what he's up to at night in his shed?"

"Probably the kind of man who spies on another man at night when he's out in his shed."

"*Observing*," said John as he helped Sarah set the table for dinner. "We're just *observing*!"

The following evening, John and Rob kept their eyes tuned sharply toward Fred's house. Their burgers and hot dogs and ribs grew cool, and their soda went flat, and questions and conversations went unanswered as their attention was rapt upon the house next door.

"Would you like some dinner?" Mary asked Rob at some point. "Or should I just set it aside for next year when you take up a new hobby?"

"Or if the spy thing doesn't work out," Sarah added.

"*Observing*," John countered. "We're *observing*!"

But Fred never came.

"What do you make of *that*?" John asked Rob late that evening as everyone packed up leftovers and headed home.

"*Strange*," Rob said. "Very *strange*. Who turns down an invitation for food?" He blinked. "Why am I still hungry?"

The following day, John and Rob met on the sidewalk in front of John's house. Their children played astronauts in the yard behind them.

"So how do we go about this?" John asked as Fred emerged from his house to check the mail. Both men smiled and waved to Fred. Fred smiled and waved back.

"We could sneak over during the day, since he seems only to be out at night," Rob suggested.

"We could ask to borrow a cup of sugar."

"We could accidentally drop something in Fred's yard and go and retrieve it."

"We could have our kids go find out."

"We could send them over with a camera."

"We could fly a mini-drone over there."

"We could purchase an insect-camera."

"Alright," Sarah said suddenly, stepping down from the front porch. She made long strides across the lawn.

"What are you doing, sweetheart?" asked John, his face paling.

"Going to put an end to this. It's Saturday morning. You two could be out enjoying the day. Instead, you're devising on your sidewalk."

"Darling, don't!"

But Sarah was already halfway to Fred.

John and Rob ducked down behind the hedge.

"What do you think she's asking him?" Rob wondered.

"The question is, *how* do you think she's asking him?" John queried. "You can't just go ask a man his business!"

"Well it's simple," said Sarah, looking over the bushes. "It's simple indeed."

"What is it?" John asked.

"He goes out there at night with his star charts and a large monitor screen and he pretends he's still flying around up there." Sarah pointed overhead. "It's like he's using a simulation program. It's kind of sweet, really."

"Sarah," John said returning to his feet, followed by Rob. "You just can't go asking a man his business."

"So I guess I won't ask you what you want for lunch."

"*That's* different."

That night, John and Sarah both watched as Fred made his way to the shed. John's breath shuddered a bit; Sarah ran her hand across his back.

"One day, I'll be that old," said John. "And I'll be forced into retirement."

"Retirement is one thing." Sarah said, kissing John's cheek. "Giving up on your dreams is another. I'll always believe in you."

John kissed his wife's fingertips and looked up toward the stars. "What do you say we take a quick step out back? See the sky the way that Fred sees it?"

A moment later, John and Sarah stood on the edge of their patio, the quiet hum of air conditioner units and the cheerful chip of crickets and the dark space surrounding them punctuated by drifting fireflies and glowing stars.

"They're beautiful, these summer nights," Sarah said.

John nodded. "But that poor man," he said at last. "I think that's what's had me so taken with the whole thing. That poor man's wife died ten years ago, thirty years below the lower end of life expectancy.

And his kids all live a few hours away. And he's here all alone with his shed."

And Sarah knew that John saw himself in Fred, the eventually-someday fate of all men.

But then all at once, the ground began a low rumble, a gentle shaking that increased every moment. John and Sarah glanced at one another. From over in Fred's yard, the shed lit up, every window and crack and unsealed space bursting with great strands and streaks of brilliant light like quasars piercing the voids of deepest space. The ground shook harder, and suddenly a roar of fire swept aside the walls and roof of the shed like dust in a strong wind. A great cloud of gray smoke rose and plumed as a cylindrical, sparkling silver rocket, inscribed with Ella, the name of Fred's late wife, leapt into the sky in a fiery trail, a light that arced higher and higher into the darkness, until it was a small light lost against the backdrop of a billion, billion stars.

And John and Sarah stood there, and held hands, and watched that singular light blink out as the ship went beyond their sight, somewhere closer to God than they stood now in that beautiful summer night.

"Retirement is one thing," John whispered the wisdom of his wife aloud, his eyes seeking out the stars in hers. "Giving up on your dreams is quite another."

ACKNOWLEDGMENTS

I don't write short stories very often. The last time I published a collection of short stories, I was eighteen. Incidentally, it was my first book. And looking back, those stories are horrible.

But I think these are better.

I have been planning this collection for a few years now, and only recently (last night as of this writing on the second day of 2016) did the last story fall into place.

If you're reading this, thank you for having read the stories. Thank you for your time and your patience.

I thank God above all for live, for beauty, for the chance to say anything at all.

I want to thank my mom, Valerie Bouthyette, and my aunt and uncle, Susan Bryant and Ed Sampiero, who patiently listened to me read the title story to them after Christmas dinner as I worked on assembling this collection. Thank you to Mom and Nancy Colna for reading through the complete collection, and returning their input and thoughts as always.

And thank you to my dog, Frankie, who always reminds me that it's time to take a break to snack or play, and who always patiently listens to the ideas I have for books.

JOE VIGLIOTTI, a native of Long Island, New York, is a writer and artist residing in northern central Maryland. He can be reached through his website at www.jvigliotti.com

Other Books by Joe Vigliotti:

Carnival Week

Return to the Shore

A Rose in February

Ghosts on the Tower

One May Weekend

The Sea in the Sky

Between Us and Rome

A Time Returned in Faith

Dark Republic

Conscience

34283918R00083

Made in the USA
Middletown, DE
15 August 2016